AVAILABLE NOW!

James Patterson's
BOOKSHOTS
Flames

THE McCULLAGH INN IN MAINE

Chelsea O'Kane escapes to Maine to build a new life—until she runs into Jeremy Holland, an old flame....

LEARNING TO RIDE

City girl Madeline Harper never wanted to love a cowboy. But rodeo king Tanner Callen might change her mind...and win her heart.

SACKING THE QUARTERBACK

Attorney Melissa St. James wins every case. Now, when she's up against football superstar Grayson Knight, her heart is on the line, too.

THE MATING SEASON

Documentary ornithologist Sophie Castle is convinced that her heart belongs only to the birds—until she meets her gorgeous cameraman, Rigg Greensman.

THE RETURN

Ashley Montoya was in love with Mack McLeroy in high school—until he broke her heart. But when an accident brings him back home to Sunnybell to recover, Ashley can't help but fall into his embrace....

'JAN - - 2018   CH

BODYGUARD

Special Agent Abbie Whitmore has only one task: protect Congressman Jonathan Lassiter from a violent cartel's threats. Yet she's never had to do it while falling in love....

DAZZLING: THE DIAMOND TRILOGY, BOOK I

To support her artistic career, Siobhan Dempsey works at the elite Stone Room in New York City...never expecting to be swept away by Derick Miller.

RADIANT: THE DIAMOND TRILOGY, BOOK II

After an explosive breakup with her billionaire boyfriend, Siobhan moves to Detroit to pursue her art. But Derick isn't ready to give her up.

EXQUISITE: THE DIAMOND TRILOGY, BOOK III

Siobhan's artistic career is finally successful, and she's ready to start a life with her billionaire boyfriend, Derick. But their relationship has been a roller-coaster ride, and Derick may not want her after all....

HOT WINTER NIGHTS

Allie Fairchild moved to Montana to start fresh as the head of the trauma center. And even though the days are cold, the nights are steamy...especially when she meets search-and-rescue leader Dex Belmont.

A WEDDING IN MAINE

Chelsea O'Kane is ready to marry Jeremy Holland in the inn they've built together—until the secrets of her past refuse to stay buried. And they could ruin everything.

BOOK**SHOTS**

CROSS KILL

Along Came a Spider killer Gary Soneji died years ago. But Alex Cross swears he sees Soneji gun down his partner. Is his greatest enemy back from the grave?

ZOO 2

Humans are evolving into a savage new species that could save civilization—or end it. James Patterson's *Zoo* was just the beginning.

THE TRIAL

An accused killer will do anything to disrupt his own trial, including a courtroom shocker that Lindsay Boxer and the Women's Murder Club will never see coming.

LITTLE BLACK DRESS

Can a little black dress change everything? What begins as one woman's fantasy is about to go too far.

THE WITNESSES

The Sanderson family has been forced into hiding after one of them stumbled upon a criminal plot. Or so they think. No one will answer their questions. And the terrifying truth may come too late....

LET'S PLAY MAKE-BELIEVE

Christy and Marty just met, and it's love at first sight. Or is it? One of them is playing a dangerous game—and only one will survive.

CHASE

A man falls to his death in an apparent accident....But why does he have the fingerprints of another man who is already dead? Detective Michael Bennett is on the case.

HUNTED

Someone is luring men from the streets to play a mysterious, high-stakes game. Former Special Forces officer David Shelley goes undercover to shut it down—but will he win?

113 MINUTES

Molly Rourke's son has been murdered. Now she'll do whatever it takes to get justice. No one should underestimate a mother's love....

$10,000,000 MARRIAGE PROPOSAL

A mysterious billboard offering $10 million to get married intrigues three single women in LA. But who is Mr. Right...and is he the perfect match for the lucky winner?

FRENCH KISS

It's hard enough to move to a new city, but now everyone French detective Luc Moncrief cares about is being killed off. Welcome to New York.

KILLER CHEF

Caleb Rooney knows how to do two things: run a food truck and solve a murder. When people suddenly start dying of food-borne illnesses, the stakes are higher than ever....

TAKING THE TITANIC

Posing as newlyweds, two ruthless thieves board the *Titanic* to rob its well-heeled passengers. But an even more shocking plan is afoot....

THE CHRISTMAS MYSTERY

Two stolen paintings disappear from a Park Avenue murder scene—French detective Luc Moncrief is in for a merry Christmas.

BLACK & BLUE

Detective Harry Blue is determined to take down the serial killer who's abducted several women, but her mission leads to a shocking revelation.

COME AND GET US

When an SUV deliberately runs Miranda Cooper and her husband off a desolate Arizona road, she must run for help alone as his cryptic parting words echo in her head: "Be careful who you trust."

PRIVATE: THE ROYALS

After kidnappers threaten to execute a royal family member in front of the Queen, Jack Morgan and his elite team of PIs have just twenty-four hours to stop them. Or heads will roll…literally.

THE HOUSE HUSBAND

Harry Posehn cooks, cleans, and takes care of the kids—until he decides that he's done being a normal stay-at-home dad. Can Detective Teaghan Beaumont catch him before it's too late?

HIDDEN

Rejected by the Navy SEALs, Mitchum is content being his small town's unofficial private eye—until his beloved fourteen-year-old cousin is abducted.

HER SECOND CHANCE AT LOVE MIGHT BE TOO GOOD TO BE TRUE....

When Chelsea O'Kane escapes to her family's inn in Maine, all she's got are fresh bruises, a gun in her lap, and a desire to start anew. That's when she runs into her old flame, Jeremy Holland. As he helps her fix up the inn, they rediscover what they once loved about each other.

Until it seems too good to last…

Read the bestselling story of hope and redemption,
The McCullagh Inn in Maine, **available now from**

A Wedding in Maine

A McCullagh Inn Story

JEN McLAUGHLIN

FOREWORD BY

JAMES PATTERSON

BookShots

Little, Brown and Company

New York Boston London

Copyright © 2017 by James Patterson
Excerpt from *A Princess in Maine* copyright © 2017 by James Patterson

Hachette Book Group supports the right to free expression and the value of copyright. The purpose of copyright is to encourage writers and artists to produce the creative works that enrich our culture.

BookShots / Little, Brown and Company
Hachette Book Group
1290 Avenue of the Americas, New York, NY 10104
bookshots.com

First Edition: January 2017

BookShots is an imprint of Little, Brown and Company, a division of Hachette Book Group, Inc. The Little, Brown name and logo are trademarks of Hachette Book Group, Inc. The BookShots name and logo are trademarks of JBP Business, LLC.

The publisher is not responsible for websites (or their content) that are not owned by the publisher.

The Hachette Speakers Bureau provides a wide range of authors for speaking events. To find out more, go to hachettespeakersbureau.com or call (866) 376-6591.

ISBN 978-0-316-50117-0
LCCN 2016943248

10 9 8 7 6 5 4 3 2

LSC-H

Printed in the United States of America

FOREWORD

When I first had the idea for BookShots, I knew that I wanted to include romantic stories. The whole point of BookShots is to give people lightning-fast reads that completely capture them for just a couple of hours in their day—so publishing romance felt right.

I have a lot of respect for romance authors. I took a stab at the genre when I wrote *Suzanne's Diary for Nicholas*. While I was happy with the results, I learned that the process of writing a romance novel required hard work and dedication.

That's why I wanted to pair up with the best romance authors for BookShots. I work with writers who know how to draw emotions out of their characters, all while catapulting their plots forward.

When I worked with Jen McLaughlin on *The McCullagh Inn in Maine*, I knew I wanted her to keep writing stories about Chelsea and Jeremy's life together. Because I'm married to my wonderful wife, Sue, I know the best moments in a relationship can come after a couple falls in love. In this book, you'll see Chelsea and Jeremy plan for the next big step…until someone tries to stop them.

James Patterson

A Wedding in Maine

A McCullagh Inn Story

Chapter 1

OUR NEWEST GUESTS had just finished signing the guest book when I walked down the front staircase. Outside, the bitter cold December night whipped snow and freezing winds against the inn, making it creak and groan, but, inside, we were safe and toasty. Jeremy took a small suitcase from the daughter—a little girl who was six years old and wearing a puffy winter coat—and looked impossibly manly with his new pink accessory. She watched him with wide eyes, clearly enamored of his easy charm.

I couldn't blame the kid. Jeremy was a bona fide hero. *My* hero.

This inn, the McCullagh Inn, had been my sanctuary when I had been on the run from an infamous drug cartel a little over a year ago. It was an inheritance from my aunt and had been the perfect place to lie low while men were gunning for me. When Jeremy, a DEA agent at the time, learned I was in trouble, he came riding to my rescue.

Jeremy watched the family go upstairs. He waited for them

to reach the top and then leaned in, his mouth a breath away from my ear. "You look absolutely stunning in that top...but I can't wait to take it off you."

My stomach tightened at the unspoken promise that deepened his voice. My man knew how to turn on the heat. I rested a hand on his hard biceps. "In that case...meet me in the back in five minutes?"

"Wouldn't miss it for the world," he said, giving me a look that was hot enough to melt my panties off in the middle of an arctic snowstorm. "To the left, Mr. and Mrs. Walter. I'm right behind you."

I smiled and waved at them as they rounded the corner, and Jeremy shot me one last heated stare before he was gone. Shivering, I wrapped my arms around myself and rubbed the goose bumps away. The Walters were our only arrivals today, so after Jeremy got them settled, it would be time for us to kick back, relax, grab a glass of wine, and just be...well, *normal*.

Normal was a magical feeling.

After being raised by a father who ran a crime circle in our small town, and then unknowingly marrying a man owned by the cartel...well, normal wasn't something I had a lot of experience with, but I was willing to learn. And Jeremy was a great tutor.

Smiling, I started my nightly rounds. We were pretty isolated out here in Hudson, with the nearest stores about a twenty-minute drive away. Behind our inn, there was a cliff that overlooked the beach and there was a forest on either side, so you would only know where we were located if you were looking for us. But despite the rural setting, I always made sure all the doors were locked, and all the windows were latched. What can I say? Life had been quiet lately, but old habits die hard. O'Kanes didn't let their guards down just because things were good. If anything, that makes us more cautious.

We protected what was ours.

Walking past the stairs that led to the guest bedrooms—completely redone by yours truly—I checked the front door. Both its walls and the picture window in the living room were new, since they had to be replaced after the drive-by shooting. Like I said, I now had a strong appreciation for normal.

I covered my mouth as I yawned, moving silently upstairs and down the hallway between the guest rooms, checking the vacant rooms to make sure the windows were closed, lights were out, part of my nightly routine that gave me a few minutes to myself. The inn was doing great. Since the grand opening in March, we had numerous bookings. It was mainly couples on romantic getaways, but the occasional family stayed here as a stop on their road trips, or for a quick run of cross-country skiing. Jeremy and I were discussing the addition of excursions or classes for the upcoming spring, but the Maine winter would hang on for another couple of months, so for now that's all it was. Talk.

Making my way back downstairs, I made a mental note to

tell Holly we had a last minute booking for the Blue Room. Jeremy and I had discovered that neither of us liked cleaning, and that we liked cleaning up after other people even *less*, so we hired Holly immediately. Her teenage brother, Henry, worked for us after school and during weekends as a bellboy/apprentice handyman. He and Holly were our only actual employees. Otherwise, we'd just call the odd cab when our guests needed transportation.

The inn was hushed when the antique grandfather clock in the living room ticked closer to ten. The living quarters I shared with Jeremy were off the kitchen, so we could grab drinks and food without traipsing through the whole inn. During renovations, Jeremy had the idea to combine two of the smaller rooms together, so we also had one larger room that functioned as a private living/dining room. It gave us plenty of privacy, especially at night when we needed it most.

But the inn was home, and generally, I preferred being out in the open with the guests.

I pushed open the staff-only door that led to the kitchen, noticing that the light was on in our living room. "Jeremy? You in there?"

No answer. Weird.

Shrugging off my sweater, I tossed it on the counter and locked the door behind me. Originally, Jeremy and I had planned to do a more traditional kitchen with white cabinets and granite countertops, but in the end, we went with a restaurant-style kitchen with gleaming stainless steel and professional gadgets. It turns out, I'm quite the cook. It was surprising to learn I could make damn good food from scratch, considering that, while growing up, I mainly ate food that came out of boxes.

Opening the door that separated our living quarters from the kitchen, I sniffed. "You in here? Hey, do I smell General Tso? I hope so. I need some—" I froze mid-sentence—*mid-step*. Death grip on the knob. Eyes wide. Heart pounding in my chest. Palms sweating. "What the hell are you doing?"

Chapter 2

JEREMY WATCHED CHELSEA pale. She looked like she was about to turn and run, and he'd expected nothing less. Chelsea and change weren't exactly the best of friends, which was why he was trying to keep this moment as low-key as possible. Still, after all the shit they'd dealt with to get where they were now, there was no doubt in his mind that this was the right move for them to make.

It was time to make this thing between them official.

Chelsea subtly turned her head from side to side, and he knew she was mapping out her most efficient exit strategy. When she got scared, her fight-or-flight instinct kicked in.

His Chelsea? Yeah. She was a runner.

But he wasn't going to let her disappear. It was time to move on to the next chapter of their lives. The happily ever after part.

"Don't go. Give me a chance to talk before you react."

She was holding the doorknob so tightly her knuckles were

white, but she wasn't making a break for it. He called that a win, thank you very damn much. "What are you doing?" she asked.

"I'm on one knee with a tiny little box in my hand, and it just happens to have a diamond ring in it. Don't read too much into it." He ran his hand through his hair, giving her his most charming and reassuring smile. "I'm just a guy, kneeling on the floor, who wants the woman he loves to spend the rest of her life with him. No big deal."

She choked on a laugh. "Not at all."

That laugh was a good starting point. "Originally, I had a big, romantic proposal in mind. Like, something in a fancy restaurant in Bangor. Maybe with a string quartet, or an opera singer, or something else ridiculously romantic. You're the best damn thing that ever happened to me, and you deserve the biggest and best of everything in the world, Chels."

She instinctively shuddered at the idea of an elaborate proposal, and he smiled, because he loved the unapologetic realist beneath those sweetest blue eyes of hers. She looked like an angel, but was tougher than steel. "Jeremy—"

"But I know you hate big, romantic gestures because you tell me they're too clichéd and a waste of time and money. So I settled on the most unromantic thing I could think of— proposing to you over cheap take-out Chinese food, in our home, after a long day at work, while wearing an old T-shirt and a ripped pair of jeans."

She tilted her head, still not letting go of the doorknob,

still looking unconvinced of this whole thing. "I like cheap Chinese food. And your ripped jeans."

"I know." Jeremy wiggled the ring box, drawing her gaze to it again. She looked so damn beautiful, standing there, almost in a full panic. "Also, I like you. A lot."

A smile played at her lips, and she tugged on a piece of her long hair and rolled her eyes in that sarcastically adorable way she always did. "Yeah, I guess you're all right, too." Her eyes widened slightly after they focused on the black box in his hand. "Is that…I saw a picture once…is it…?"

"Your mother's ring?" He glanced down. It was a princess cut diamond, and the band had tiny little diamonds all around it. It sparkled in the light from their bedroom chandelier in a way that was stunning and majestic. Most importantly, it meant something special to Chelsea, and he'd do anything to make her eyes sparkle, too. "Yes. I went to ten different pawn shops in Maine trying to find it. Paul told me your dad hocked it a while back, but wasn't sure when or where." Well. At least that was what Paul had said after Jeremy badgered him for information. They weren't exactly the best of friends. "I knew I only had a shot in hell finding it, but luckily, it never sold, and I found it in Bangor at a pawn shop of questionable legality."

"Sounds like Dad's type of place." Chelsea finally released the knob, her body relaxing with the movement. This was the moment of truth. Jeremy held his breath, waiting to see if she'd retreat or come closer. "You did all of that for me?"

"I'd do anything for you." He resisted the urge to groan when she took a step toward him, then stopped. "There's no doubt in my mind that we're destined to spend the rest of our lives together. I've lived a life without you for too damn long and I have no intention of ever going back. You've made me the happiest man alive, and I believe everything we've been through led us to this moment. Let me spend the rest of my life making you as happy as you've made me. Marry me, Chels."

"That wasn't a question," she said, taking another step toward him.

Damn right it wasn't a question. He had spent way too many years as her friend, utterly blind to the fact that they loved each other. It wasn't until she left town, disappearing without a trace, that he'd realized the truth. Once they reconnected, once he had her back in his arms, he knew he was never going to let her go. That was never going to change.

"I'm not asking," Jeremy said. It may not have been a question, but he felt like his entire life hung on her answer. Even the inn itself seemed to hold its breath with him, waiting. "I love you. Marry me, Chels."

She crossed the room, stopping in front of him. He was eye-level with her stomach, so he tipped his head back to meet her gaze. She looked so damn gorgeous, standing there, with that quizzical look, as her fear had seemed to fade into bemusement. She pushed her hair back off her face and the chipped nail polish on her fingernails danced in cheerful spurts of lilac against her pale skin. Then she smiled. "If it's not a question, am I still supposed to answer?"

In the DEA, Jeremy had learned to read the slightest nuance in body language and could decipher the meaning behind the smallest facial tic. With Chelsea, though, he didn't need any of those tricks. There was no one in the world he knew better. Looking at her now, seeing the look in her eyes, the way she held her lips together, he knew.

"Yeah." His heart pounded so hard and fast it echoed in his head. His pulse surged into the danger zone. "Go ahead."

"Okay. How's this for an answer?" She dropped to her knees, cupped his face, and smiled, her eyes watering in a rare display of sentimentality. "I love you. I loved you before I understood what love was, and I will love you until the day I die. I want to spend the rest of my life with you, in this inn, building a future together. You and me, always."

He smiled, curling a hand behind the nape of her neck, under all that soft brown hair he loved so damn much. Every dream he had suddenly came true and a million more burst into being as she smiled at him, adoration written on her face. Lowering his head, he stopped just short of kissing her. "So, to make sure I understand, that's a yes?"

She nodded once. "That's a *hell* yes."

Letting out a small laugh, he melded his mouth to hers, sealing her response with a kiss. Chelsea was his, and he was hers, and nothing would ever change that.

Not even the devil himself.

Chapter 3

THE SECOND HIS lips touched mine, I knew that he was in complete and utter control, and I had absolutely no problem with that. I was fiercely independent to the point of obtuse stubbornness, but when it came to Jeremy and his possessive touches that roamed all over my body, I willingly gave myself over to him every time. I wasn't a romantic. I was a cynic, especially since the last Prince Charming I found turned out to be pure evil. But being with Jeremy made me believe that happy endings did exist. With Jeremy, if you tried to be a good person, good things would happen to you. Good things like Jeremy fricking Holland.

He gently lowered me to the carpeted floor, and as he shifted between my thighs, my shirt bunched up at the small of my back. He caught it tightly in his fist. Our mouths perfectly melded together and his tongue touched mine, drawing an animalistic moan from me. His palm closed over my breast and I arched my back, my pulse quickening when he dragged the side of his thumb over my nipple. He broke the kiss off abruptly, burying his face in my neck, and kissing the spot directly over my pulse so gently I almost missed it. "Not yet."

I blinked, my stomach a tight knot of need. I had no idea what game he was playing, but if he didn't please me soon he was about to have one pissed-off fiancée on his hands. Fiancée. God. I was Jeremy Holland's *fiancée*. Till death do us part. The urge to run tried to resurface, but I shoved it down. "What?"

He pushed up, shifting onto his knees. Picking up the ring box, he took the stunner of a ring, my mother's ring, out. Holding it between his thumb and pointer finger, he smiled down at me. "Before I make you scream my name, this needs to be on your finger."

Slowly, I balanced myself on an elbow and held my left hand out. My pulse was racing. He slid the ring on my finger reverently, and I held my breath as I stared down at it, wiggling my finger experimentally. It fit me perfectly. Of course.

Jeremy would have made sure of that.

My boyfriend—*fiancé*—was nothing if not a perfectionist.

I didn't say anything, mostly because I was filled with so much emotion I could barely *breathe*. It was a weird mixture of excitement and hope, with a healthy dash of reality. The idea that my father could have loved my mother enough to give her a ring like this was unsettling. He never talked about her much while I was growing up. What had happened to make them fall apart? And, more importantly…would something like that happen to me and Jeremy?

There wasn't much that scared me. Give me bullets flying at my head or a murderous drug cartel, and I did what I had to do to survive. I fought back until I won. But the idea of loving and losing Jeremy? Yeah. That scared me more than anything.

"Hey." He caught my chin. "What's wrong?"

"Nothing," I said quickly, curling my hand into a fist and resting it back on the carpet. "Nothing's wrong at all."

He hesitated, before lowering himself back onto me, propping himself up on his forearms to keep his weight off me. He cupped my cheek, resting his thumb on the bottom of my chin. "You don't have to hide anything from me. Not anymore, Chels. If you're not ready, we can just take it off and go back to—"

"I'm ready," I interrupted, resting a hand on his heart. It sped up under my touch, like it always did. I loved that. Loved how he held nothing back from me.

"If you're sure."

I trailed my hand down his chest, over his abs, and teased his impressive bulge, straining against his jeans to be set free. I was the perfect girl for the job. "I'm *very* sure."

Eyes darkening with desire, he slid his hand under my butt, pulling me against his erection possessively, his grip unyielding yet gentle. "Now. Where were we…?"

I closed my fingers over his hard length, squeezing with the perfect amount of pressure. I wanted to make him as crazy as he made me. "Right. Here."

He growled and slammed his mouth down on mine,

taking my breath away in the most delicious way possible. From the second he kissed me, everything he did was calculated to drive me closer to the edge. He was a mad scientist, and I was his willing test subject. A fingernail dragged across my nipple as he took off my shirt and bra. A squeeze on my butt as he removed my pants. A brush of his fingertips across my clit as he peeled my panties down my legs. Every few seconds, a torturous stoke of his fingers on my overheated skin.

By the time he had me naked, I was a trembling, tangled ball of impatient need, and there was only one cure for that. Jeremy *fricking* Holland.

When I gripped his shirt, he allowed me to end the kiss long enough to tear it over his head, and then we were kissing again as I undid his jeans. The second I had them pulled down, he lifted himself up and kicked out of them. Then he was blessedly naked.

I grinned against his mouth. "I see it's a no underwear day."

He chuckled. It was the sexiest sound I ever heard. He occasionally went without boxers, because it was a way "to keep me guessing all day long." And it worked. Many quickies had started so I could satisfy my curiosity. I lifted my chin, seeking another kiss, but instead Jeremy lowered himself down my body, leaving a trail of love bites as he made his way to my belly. When he nipped the skin directly over the small patch of curls between my legs, I closed my eyes.

"Chelsea…" He caught my hand, the one with the ring,

and entwined his fingers with mine. "I love you so damn much."

Before I could say *I love you, too,* his mouth was on me, and two fingers of his free hand thrust inside me. I was beyond words or thoughts, and wasn't capable of anything more than a strangled groan. I closed my thighs on either side of his head, lifting my hips and moving against him with a frantic need I didn't bother to hide.

There were no secrets between us.

Every nerve in my body pulled taut until I came with crystal clear clarity. Pleasure rolled over my body, making my limbs weak. I was breathing heavily as he lifted my leg fluidly, resting my ankle against his shoulder, and thrust deep inside me. It felt so good that I legit *screamed* his name. Just like he'd wanted.

Smirking, he lowered his hand to my mouth, and covered it with a questioning brow. I nodded, because there was no way I was going to be quiet tonight, and we had guests. Grunting, he moved, driving me insane with so much pleasure I was sure I was going to *die*. I lost track of how many times he made me come, but when he pressed a finger against my clitoris as he drove inside me a final time, I came in tandem with him, crying out against his hand as he collapsed on top of me with a long, dragged-out groan.

In this moment, life was the best it had been in…well, ever.

Being in love might be corny and cliché, but it was also pretty fricking awesome. Every dark moment, every shitty experience, every bleeding cut life had given me, had all been worth it because it brought me here, to Jeremy and the bright future ahead of us. Right now, life couldn't get any better—

But then there was a crash outside the door, and we both froze.

Chapter 4

JEREMY WAS INSTANTLY up on his feet, tossing a blanket over my naked body, and had stepped into his pants before I could even blink. There were those ninja DEA moves I'd almost forgotten about. He started for the door. After glancing at me to make sure I was covered, he opened the door to the kitchen. "Hello? Mr. Walters?"

As soon as he closed the door, I yanked my shirt over my head and pulled my pants on. By the time the door opened again, I was dragging my hands through my hair, trying to mold it into the "messy beach waves" style rather than the "wild bedroom sex" look I was currently rocking. I failed miserably.

Jeremy shut the door and leaned against it, dragging a hand down his face as he let out a small laugh. "False alarm. No one was out there."

I walked over to him, my bare feet silent on the carpet. "I swear I heard something."

"I did, too, but I found a box of cereal on the floor in front of the fridge. Maybe it fell?" He shrugged, reaching out one arm to put a hand on my hip and tug me closer.

"Maybe…" I could have sworn the sound was louder than cardboard hitting tile. You know what they say: you're not paranoid if they really *are* out to get you. In my experience, someone was *always* out to get me. Why should that be any different, simply because I was happy now? "The kitchen door was still locked?"

"Yep. And you know you checked the front door. You always do." Jeremy pulled me into his arms reassuringly, my hands sliding along the bare skin of his back. "We're alone, Chels."

Logically, I knew he was right, but a tendril of a memory from my past kept sneaking its way into my mind, rousing my worry. "Did you check the windows, too?"

"Yep. All secured." Jeremy walked me backward, guiding me to our bedroom, but I was unable to shake the uneasiness creeping up my spine. "There's no one back here but you and me, and that's the way I like it."

"Do you now?" I knew he was trying to reignite the celebratory mood, so I did my best to let my unsettled emotions go. Raising my arms to drape them around his neck, I sidled closer.

"Oh, yeah," he said, his voice dropping sexily low as he slid his hands over my butt, caressing it seductively.

In the next moment, we were making out again. We headed back to the bedroom and by the time we came back up for air, I was completely spent and satisfied. We curled up in bed together, my head on his shoulder, and my left hand on his heart. With a sigh, he played with my hair like he always did before he fell asleep. I stared at the motionless blades of the ceiling fan as I tried to stay in the moment.

He stopped playing with my hair so he could trace the cut of the diamond in my ring, and my heart warmed at the soft, almost reverent, way he looked at it. My eyelids lowered, and I yawned, shifting around until I found the perfect spot, curled up against his body. The steady thump of his heartbeat coaxed me into a state of relaxation.

"What do you think about a winter wedding?" he asked, his voice rumbly and low, disrupting the haze of near-sleep that had settled over me like a warm blanket.

"Huh?" I was normally a night person, but my stomach was growling so hard I couldn't think. It had been a long day, filled with excitement and lots of sex.

I got up and headed to the living room, where our Chinese food was still ready for us.

Jeremy followed me in and kept the conversation going. "Like, February," he said slowly. "Maybe…February 11th?"

I popped a piece of chicken in my mouth and turned so I could see his face. "Of next year, you mean?"

"No. Like…in two months." Jeremy smiled as his fingertips brushed my bare shoulder, lost in a dream world where weddings were magically pulled together in a few weeks. "I want to marry you, Chels. What's the point in planning some huge, elaborate wedding when between the two of us, we have one family member to invite?"

I choked on a laugh, because, God, he was right. His parents were dead and he didn't have any siblings or extended family. I only had my brother and my incarcerated father—who wouldn't have been invited no matter what his current legal status was. "Wow. We're pathetic," I said. "We're only going to have one person at our wedding."

He laughed, touching the tip of my nose playfully. "Maybe. Maybe not."

"What's that supposed to mean?" I asked, frowning, pushing his finger away.

"There's your father. I suppose we could wait for him to get released, so he can walk you down the aisle." He studied me. "If you want him to."

My father and I…we had a difficult relationship, to put it lightly.

Johnny O'Kane believed you looked out for your family, and took advantage of everyone else. When he bothered to be around at all, he'd raised Paul and me to follow in his footsteps. With me, it didn't take, and I became an assistant DA in Miami instead. I didn't want to follow his criminal career path. So the idea of him walking me down the aisle, like a *normal* dad, didn't exactly fill me with the warm and fuzzies. In fact, it made me queasy. "No. No way."

"Okay," he said, smiling at me. "Then we don't wait. We do it our way at the courthouse with the two of us and Paul."

And that's when I realized there was a part of me—a small, long-denied part of me—that *did* stupidly want the fairy-tale wedding. I wanted to walk down the aisle toward Jeremy. I wanted to see him waiting for me with a big, sappy grin. And maybe, just maybe, I'd make him cry with the sheer force of my beauty. That small part of me was loud, but I tried my best to ignore it as it wept into its imaginary bouquet, all alone at the back of the imaginary aisle I'd never walk.

That version of me was annoying, unrealistic, and *soft*.

A courthouse wedding was easy, cheap, and practical. Surely it was the best way to go. Right?

"Okay," I agreed.

After we finished eating, we laid back down, and I rested my head on his shoulder again. I'd been quiet ever since he suggested the courthouse wedding, and I could tell he was curious as to why, but he kept silent, letting me work through it. My engagement ring caught the light of the bedside lamp, and I closed my eyes. As I drifted off to sleep in my fiancé's arms, an idea…a fricking *crazy* idea…popped inside my mind. Knowing he was almost asleep, I whispered, "On second thought, I might want a different wedding. Maybe something involving the inn. Wanna talk about it tomorrow morning?"

"Of course. It's you and me, Chels, you and me."

As sleep beckoned, visions of poufy white dresses, delicate pink flowers, and Jeremy's proud smile at the altar danced in my head. Okay, yes, it was all sappy and corny, but I'd just gotten engaged. If there was ever a time to dream of a fairy tale and a happy ending, it was today. The strains of the "Wedding March" was my lullaby as I sank into slumber.

Chapter 5

THE NEXT MORNING, I cracked open the window in the kitchen to let in the smell of the brisk ocean breeze. I liked cold, liked the way it opened up your lungs and froze the tip of your nose until you couldn't feel it anymore. I held a full mug of steaming caramel coffee, inhaled its fresh aroma, and let my eyes close in relaxation. This was my favorite time of day, early in the morning when no one else was awake, before I had to worry about cooking breakfast for the guests.

My habit of waking early in the morning had started back when I was a kid. It wasn't an enjoyable choice, not back then, but if I wanted to eat a healthy breakfast and pack school lunches for me and Paul, I had to do it myself. My father, if he was around, would still be asleep and his "business associates" would all be gone. The house would be quiet. Peaceful.

I learned to treasure those moments of peace.

There was a faint *clink* as I readjusted my grip on the mug and I glanced down. My engagement ring. Excited butterflies took off in my stomach, because the crazy ideas I'd had last night before falling asleep had hatched into a fully developed plan overnight. The corner of my mouth tipped up into an involuntary smile. I still couldn't believe Jeremy proposed…or that I'd said yes so readily. If I was dreaming, don't pinch me. I never wanted to wake up again.

I preferred this happy oblivion to cold hard reality, anyway.

Jeremy came into the kitchen, yawning and running his hands through his mussed hair. "Morning, sunshine."

"Good morning."

"The Walters got an early start. They decided to go hiking, and watch the sun rise over the ocean. Won't be back until dinnertime." He headed over to the coffee machine. "They left a note on the check-in desk. I saw it when I got the paper."

"Oh. Good." I pressed a hand to my fluttering stomach. "That gives us time to talk about the wedding."

"Yup." He took a sip of his coffee, cursing under his breath because it was too hot—*duh*—and then mumbled, "I should probably make this an Irish coffee."

My fiancé, folks, the comedian innkeeper. "Do whatever you want, but then get your butt over here. We have to talk."

"Last time you had that look in your eye, I ended up on the roof, early in the morning, ripping off shingles." He topped off his coffee, avoiding the whiskey, and settled across from me. He rested his foot on the bottom rungs of my chair, in between mine, like he did every morning. "What's up?"

"I was thinking.…We fell in love here. Rediscovered each other here. True, we slept together that one time when we were younger, but when we first made love again, it was right here in this inn."

Jeremy cocked his head toward the front of the house, where the stairs led up to my old bedroom. "I know. I was there. It was one of my finest efforts."

I rolled my eyes at his cheesy humor. "This is our home. Our life. Our everything." I took a deep breath and held it in, trying to calm my racing heart.

He stared at me. "I'm getting nervous. Why are you saying all this? If you changed your mind…"

"I want a real wedding. A fancy one. And a gorgeous wedding dress, all lacy and fluffy, with a long veil." I blurted out. "And flowers. Lots of flowers."

He blinked at me in surprise. I think he would have looked less shocked if I told him I thought high heels were the greatest human invention. "What?"

"I'm saying…I want *the* wedding. And we should have it here, in the inn. A huge, lavish, affair. And we should invite the entire town to see it all."

"Funny," he said, chuckling.

I said nothing. He'd realize I was serious eventually.

He made a sudden choking sound, before lowering his mug with a frown. He checked out the room, as if he thought I had a hidden camera pointed at him or something. "Wait. You're being serious?"

"Yes." I reached across the table and caught his hand. "I know it's silly, but I want a real wedding ceremony and reception."

"It's not silly at all," he said quickly. "Anything you want, it's yours. You know that. I just didn't think you'd want to do all that elaborate stuff."

"It's going to be time-consuming," I admitted. "It's completely out of our comfort zone, having the wedding here, but that's how we roll. We do crazy stuff and hope it works out, and so far it has. We already have honeymooners staying with us. Why not do a big, elaborate wedding to show the locals how amazing the inn would be as a venue?"

He cocked his head. "Wait. You want to push the inn as a wedding venue?"

"Weddings. Bar mitzvahs. Formal events."

His eyes lit up with understanding. "So this is basically a marketing pitch."

I looked away before grabbing hold of my courage with both hands. "Look, I know I'm not normally one for the girly stuff, but when I was a little girl, I imagined getting married. Every girl wants that one special day where you get to leave your ordinary life behind and become a princess. I used to go through my parents' wedding album, dreaming over all the photos, until my father caught me one day and, well…"

The table suddenly became the most fascinating thing in the room and Jeremy reached over to take my hand, his thumb brushing my engagement ring. My mother's ring.

"That's how I recognized the ring. And the fact that you actually found it, it's like a sign. The beginning of a fairy tale, you know? Getting to showcase the inn, it's an added bonus."

My heart sped up with excitement. "We'll invite the town here. Show them what we can do. Blow them away. Cement ourselves as a premier party location. Book a bunch of weddings. Easy peasy."

He frowned. "But neither of us has any experience party-planning, and two months is hardly enough time to pull off the wedding you're suggesting. I get your thought process, and I want to make this happen for you, but we don't need to kill ourselves for a winter wedding. I mentioned that before you told me all this. If we're going to do this, and do it right, then we need to take our time and make it perfect."

"The thing is," I said, sighing—and I could practically feel the stars in my eyes—"when I was little, I dreamed of a winter wedding. The white in the snow, the white in my dress…"

Jeremy raised a questioning brow, and I didn't blame him. I definitely didn't sound like myself right now.

I took a breath and continued. "Besides, if we don't have a winter wedding we'll miss out on bookings, and the revenue it could bring us," I said, point-blank. "Yes, I want the fairy tale, but so does everyone else. Normal people book their venues a year or more in advance, so the longer we push off the wedding, the longer it'll be before we can start locking in events."

He rubbed his chin, his forehead creased like it always did when he was thinking something over intently. I kept my face impassive and patiently waited for him to see that I was right. I know to never bet anything I can't afford to lose, but I also know that I'll never win big if I always play it safe. This plan was crazy, but it was the kind of crazy a girl like me thrived on, and my gut was screaming at me to go for it. So was my inner child, that lonely little girl who was finally getting her Prince Charming.

"Okay," he finally said. "I would marry you in a cardboard box under a bridge with rats as our guests if you wanted me to, so if you want to have a big wedding here, in the place that brought us together again, with all the poufs and frills, I'm on board. All I want is you."

"Really?" I smiled, catching his hand, my heart racing for a whole other reason...like how he was looking at me as if it'd be only a matter of minutes before he was buried inside me.

He rested his finger on the back of my mother's—no, *my* ring, and leaned closer. "Yep. I think it's a great idea, Chels."

"I'm so happy! But with that said?" I pulled my hand free, and picked my laptop up from the empty chair next to me, doing my best to ignore his sexy bedroom eyes. "It's time to start planning. I've already started a tentative list of bakers, caterers, and florists you have to visit today. Get your computer, too. I sent you the Google doc."

Jeremy groaned dramatically. I got to enjoy the view of his mighty fine ass as he padded out of the room to fetch his laptop. He re-entered, with his laptop and an exaggerated pout. "I should've gotten the whiskey."

I pointed a playful finger at him. "Once we manage to pull this off, the McCullagh Inn will be the premier wedding destination in northern Maine, and you'll be thankful for my hit-the-ground-running organization skills."

"I'm always thankful for you and your skills. Just not necessarily this early in the morning." He opened his computer, yawning again. "That's weird."

"What? What's wrong?"

"Nothing. It's just…" He pushed a button on the keyboard. "My computer was shut off improperly, so it's rebooting now. I never do that. I always let it power down before I close it."

My hands froze on the keyboard as his words sank in. "I thought that mine had been moved. Just to the left of where I left it on my desk, but it was enough for me to notice." The cursor jiggered wildly across the screen as my fingers tapped nervously on the laptop's touchpad. "Do you think it means something?"

Jeremy glanced at my computer, then his, and shook his head. "I doubt it. Maybe Mr. or Mrs. Walters tried to check their email before they left on their hike, and shut it down when they realized it was password protected. I'm sure it's nothing."

I wanted to believe him, but my sixth sense was screaming that something was going on, and it had never been wrong before. To be fair, sometimes I didn't listen to it until I was forced to shoot my way out of a situation, but still. It was never *wrong*.

"Chels." He pushed the computer aside and came around the table, catching my hand and helping me stand. "It's fine. Everything's fine. We're happy. We have nothing to worry about."

"That's the problem," I muttered. The wind picked up, the frozen tree branches suddenly bending from the force, mirroring the downward turn in my mood.

His brow furrowed, and he stared down at me. "I don't follow."

"We're happy. Stupid happy. Like smiling for no reason happy. Dancing around in your bedroom happy. Singing off-key in the shower happy."

He laughed. "I might sing off-key, but you don't."

"True." Hard to admit, but I have a pretty good voice. He wasn't just saying that because he was stupidly in love with me. "But—"

"Why is being happy a bad thing?" he interrupted gently. "I like being happy with you."

"Me, too." I gripped the front of his shirt, not letting go. "But when things are too good, they have a way of turning south really fast. When things are good, that's when shit gets blown apart. It's the way the world works. It balances itself out."

"Not with us." He ran his thumb over my lower lip, pressing on it gently. "We already paid our dues. We had the bad before the good. Nothing is going to happen to ruin—"

Knock, knock, knock.

I lifted a brow. "You were saying?"

Chapter 6

THE FATES COULDN'T resist screwing with him, could they? Okay, to be honest, Jeremy wasn't entirely convinced that Chelsea didn't have a point about the laptops. But with no proof, he was keeping mum on the subject. She had enough to worry about without them chasing their own shadows around. They were about to plan an epic wedding in a very short amount of time, something that had amazingly been *her* idea, and the last thing she needed was more stress.

The timing of that knock, though, seemed to underscore Chelsea's feeling that the proverbial shoe was about to drop on their heads. And right now? It felt more like a damn anvil.

"I know you see me as an incredibly handsome and buff superhero, but I actually don't have the power to see the future," Jeremy quipped, trying to break the blanket of tension that had dropped on the room. "And neither do you."

As he hoped, Chelsea rolled her eyes at his joke. "All right, then," she said. "Let's go see who knocked."

He followed her through the kitchen, passing the dining

room with its pale, golden-yellow walls. Rather than having one large table in the room, they'd set up four smaller tables for their guests who chose to eat here instead of ordering room service. The crystal chandelier overhead gleamed, catching stray beams of light, in a testament to Holly's cleaning skills. Everything in this inn had been handpicked by him and Chelsea.

The front door opened before they reached it, and Jeremy lowered his hand out of instinct, reaching for the butt of a gun that wasn't there. Now that he was no longer a DEA agent, he kept his weapon in the gun safe, as he'd assumed guests wouldn't warm to armed innkeepers. Besides, he was happy with his new occupation in life. Sure, he'd loved the adrenaline rush he'd gotten when working on a DEA assignment when he was young, but now that he was with Chelsea, he was ready to settle down. Take it slow.

He shifted in front of Chelsea, and she gave him a little push, but didn't move.

"Hello?" It was Paul, sticking his head inside. "Anyone home?"

Jeremy relaxed his stance only slightly. While Paul was trying to clean up his act, his shoes were still dirty as hell. "Yeah."

"Oh. Hi."

The imaginary threat gone, Chelsea shifted to Jeremy's side, leaning against him. He automatically wrapped his arm around her.

"We need to talk," Paul said, talking to Chelsea but glancing at Jeremy from the corner of his eye. The two men had an uneasy truce. Paul was grateful for the way Jeremy had protected his sister when things had gone down with the cartel, but he was never going to be comfortable around the law, even if the murky part of his life was in the past. But Jeremy's instincts told him Paul was still hiding secrets. Lots and lots of secrets. And secrets meant Paul couldn't be trusted. "Alone. It's about Dad."

Jeremy stayed silent. He didn't want to leave because he had a vested interest in keeping Chelsea safe and happy, but if she asked him to go, he'd respect her wishes. Since history had a habit of repeating itself, chances were news about her father would *not* make her happy. Whatever information Paul brought? It wouldn't be good.

Chelsea tensed. "What about him?"

"We should discuss this alone," Paul repeated.

"I can wait in the kitchen," Jeremy said gently, squeezing her hand reassuringly before letting go. "It's okay."

She caught his fingers. "No, it's not. We're getting married. Anything he has to say to me, he can say to you, too. It's not like you're a fed anymore."

"You said yes?" Paul asked, glancing at the ring on her finger. "Seriously?"

She lifted her chin. "Did you seriously think I wouldn't?"

"Dad always said—"

"I don't care what Dad says anymore."

"Clearly." Paul crossed his arms, finally looking away from

her ring finger. "But that might change soon. He's getting out early for good behavior."

"So the prisons are full again," Chelsea said dryly. Johnny O'Kane was *never* on "good behavior." She glanced at Jeremy. "And there it is."

He stiffened, because, damn it, she was right. "Maybe."

"There what is?" Paul asked, frowning.

"The bad news. I knew some was coming."

"It doesn't have to be bad," Paul retorted, shooting Jeremy a dirty look, as if *he* was responsible for their father being a shithead. "Dad wants to see you. When he heard you were back, and the inn had reopened, he lit up like a Molotov cocktail."

Only an O'Kane would use that analogy instead of saying he lit up like a light bulb. Or something else equally benign.

"No. Absolutely not," Chelsea said, shaking her head.

Paul pressed his mouth into a hard line. Honestly, Jeremy couldn't blame him for his loyalty to his father. After Chelsea had fled from town, Johnny had been the only family Paul had left. "You need to give him a chance. Maybe he's changed."

"You say that every time he gets out. You do realize that he spent more time breaking the law than being our father? And the few times he did remember he had kids, he was a jackass to us," she pointed out, logically.

Jeremy turned his attention out the window. The wind was blowing snow off the branches. He sympathized with the wind. He wanted to push something off its perch, namely Paul. Then he and Chelsea could go back to living in their happy little bubble.

"He always remembers us," Paul snapped. "*You're* the one who forgets."

Chelsea said nothing.

Jeremy turned to look at her, frowning when he saw she'd become visibly upset. It wasn't like her to show her emotions so damn clearly. "Are you all right?"

Chelsea nodded, not speaking.

"Of course she's all right." Paul shot him an incredulous look before turning back to Chelsea. "Look, he's our father and you—"

"She said no," Jeremy finally snapped. *Shit.* Now that he'd interjected himself into the conversation, there was no way in hell he was leaving it. Normally, he knew Chelsea could take care of herself, but Paul was her big brother. "I like you, man, but you need to let it go."

Paul ignored him, but his nostrils flared with anger, giving away the fact that he'd heard Jeremy perfectly well. "So Dad wants to see you. I'll bring him by when I pick him up. You don't even have to leave home."

"No," Chelsea said, shifting closer to Jeremy. "Drop it, Paul."

Paul frowned at the way she was leaning on Jeremy, clearly not liking it. "But—"

Jeremy threw an arm over her shoulder, shooting Paul a

hard glance. "You heard her the first ten times, man. Back off, or I'll help you back off."

"This is between me and my sister," Paul shot back, fisting his hands at his sides. It didn't take a genius to know he was itching for a fight. While Chelsea dealt with her childhood issues by creating a tough exterior she often hid behind, Paul was a hothead with an anger problem. When Paul was upset, he'd walk into a bar and a brawl would erupt moments later. "Why don't you get back on your white horse and ride out of here, *cop?*"

Jeremy gritted his teeth, but didn't rise to the bait.

"Don't call him that. He's not in the DEA anymore," Chelsea said, her voice low.

Paul shrugged. "Once a cop, always a cop."

"Stop trying to pick a fight with my fiancé," Chelsea snapped, clearly not giving a shit about their silent standoff. "Paul, I love you, you're always welcome here, but I have no interest in seeing our father again. Tell him to stay away. *Far* away."

Paul met his sister's steady gaze and rolled his shoulders uncomfortably. Finally he unclenched his fists, and crossed his arms. "He's not going to listen."

"Then he'll find out what happens when he breaks into our home," she said, as she headed for the kitchen. "Bye, Paul."

The second they were alone, Paul stepped forward, his jaw tight, body trembling visibly with a pent-up anger. "You may have convinced my sister to marry you, but that just means you'll have to decide where your loyalties lie. With us…or the law."

Chapter 7

A WEEK AFTER Paul broke the news about our father's early release, I was still on edge. For the last seven days, little things had been setting off alarms for me. Nothing huge, just a paper out of place here. A drawer left open there. My keys out of their usual place. They were little things that, on their own, meant nothing. But when put together…

Yeah. I didn't like it.

The way Jeremy was acting didn't help any. I could tell that he was on edge, too, but he put on a good face, always taking an optimistic view, no matter how often I told him otherwise. Of course, I could read him and I knew he was trying to keep me from stressing out even more, especially since the wedding preparations had kicked into gear.

Jeremy was currently in town, picking up the supplies I'd told him to purchase at the local crafts store. We were going to try our hand at making our own wedding centerpieces, modeled after something I'd seen on the engaged girl's best friend…Pinterest.

I was crazy about these bowls with romantic candles. They were simple and elegant, and looked easy enough for the two of us to make. Despite my ingrained realism and practical nature, settling into this creative outlet felt like heaven. I was loving every bit of wedding planning. Thriving on it, some might even say.

Over the years I'd learned to play the tough girl, but right now, I wished I could send a letter back to the little girl I used to be—the one who'd had to watch that photo album burn—and let her know that it was okay to hope for something better.

Maybe I could help lots of brides-to-be make their dreams come true at this very inn, and maybe I could make a lot of money in the process, satisfying both the realist and the dreamer in me.

But for now, I was in the office, surrounded by piles of to-do lists and wedding magazines. Appointments had been set to meet with Georgia, the owner of the local bakery, for the wedding cake, and also with Hannah, a local photographer, who came highly recommended. I still had to pick out the best array of seasonal flowers, decide on the menu, and, most importantly, find my wedding dress. My white, poufy, *girly* wedding dress.

I couldn't wait.

Next week's appointment at Wedding Belles couldn't come soon enough.

I was typing in a florist website when suddenly, there was a distant *thud*. I froze, pulse racing, because I was completely alone in the inn. The Walters had checked out, and the next batch of guests weren't expected until Friday.

Who the hell was here?

Standing silently, I crept out into the entryway, grabbing the wooden baseball bat that had been my constant companion lately. I palmed it, knowing that I was probably overreacting, but another part of me was sure I was about to walk into some kind of real-life nightmare. I slowly checked the other rooms on the first floor, making my way back to our private rooms. Nothing seemed unusual until I reached our bedroom.

The closet looked like it had been torn apart; shoes and old clothes were spilling out onto the hardwood floor. Hangers were askew. A box containing the old sports equipment lay on its side with the handle of a tennis racket poking through the flaps. Something glinted in the sunlight in the middle of the floor, framed by one of my old pair of jeans. I made my way over to it. When I saw what it was, my stomach dropped.

I hadn't laid eyes on that necklace in almost a year. Seeing it brought me back to the last time I wore it, on my desperate escape to Maine from Miami. After all, Richard had given it to me.

Who would care about an expensive necklace my ex-boyfriend had given me? Did someone break in looking for something to steal? Or worse—was it a message?

Richard had to be back.

That explained everything strange that was going on. Richard had escaped from jail. For me.

I should have shot him dead when I had the chance.

Looking wildly around the room, I searched for another indicator Richard had been here. Maybe the cartel was after me again.

Hesitantly, I took a step forward. My foot hit something hard, nudging it free from under one of Jeremy's college sweatshirts. It took a few seconds before I recognized the broken remains of the closet shelf.

I laughed at myself, rubbing my chest as I let the bat drop to the floor. Maybe Jeremy was right, maybe I was freaking out over nothing. Maybe the stress of wedding planning was starting to get to me. I was imagining monsters hiding in the closet. I must have shoved the necklace into my jeans' pocket at some point, and it had fallen out when the closet shelf broke.

Picking up the bat and resting it against my shoulder, I surveyed the mess, strategizing the best place to start reorganizing it, when someone grabbed my other shoulder from behind.

Swallowing a scream, I spun, swinging the bat as I pivoted on my heel, putting my whole weight behind it. Richard! He *was* back. If he was trying to mess with my happy ending, then I was going to finish him. And this time?

I'd make sure there was no possibility of another resurrection.

Chapter 8

JEREMY CAUGHT THE end of the bat. His eyes were wide and he stumbled back from the force of Chelsea's blow. His palm stung from the contact. She could have broken his finger, and, *Jesus,* it seemed she was trying to kill him.

When she realized the bat was no longer a viable weapon, she threw herself at him, taking them both to the floor. They landed in a heap of legs and arms, and then she lifted her fist. If he wasn't careful, she was going to break his nose like she had back in high school, when she'd claimed she "accidentally" hit him with a baseball in gym class.

"Chels!"

She froze, breathing heavily, blinking, straddling his body. After she focused on him, she frowned, her face flushed with exertion and adrenaline. "Jeremy?"

"Yeah. It's me." He held his hands out, showing her he wasn't a threat, because she was still in fight mode, and it would take her a second to come down. "What happened?"

"I thought you were Richard."

"Richard is in jail," he said slowly.

Chelsea slid to the side to sit and bring up her knees, burying her face in her arms. "Yeah, and he was dead before, but he came back, didn't he? Why would jail stop him when a bullet didn't?"

She had a point. For the first time, he registered the mess in their bedroom and, given all the other weird shit that had happened, Jeremy was officially worried. If Richard had somehow managed to escape prison or if the cartel was back in their lives…he pushed off the floor in one smooth motion. "Stay here. Keep the bat. Call 911 if you hear fighting."

She sat up. "Jer—"

He was gone before she had a chance to finish his name. The chances of Richard being in their inn were slim to none, but when it came to Chelsea's safety, there was no such thing as being too careful. After a quick search of the inn, Jeremy concluded that nothing was broken, stolen, or out of place. And yet…

Someone had been here.

He could feel it.

Chelsea wasn't the type to panic over nothing, so if she thought she was in danger, then he believed her. Someone was messing with his girl, and that meant he needed to make sure that Richard was still locked away behind bars.

Jeremy headed back to their bedroom and met Chelsea in the kitchen. She was leaning against a counter, sipping a glass of whiskey. He went to her, wrapping an arm around her hips. "I see you listened to me?"

She leaned her head against his chest, ignoring his sarcastic statement. "I didn't hear any fighting, so I guess you didn't find anyone?"

"No." He tucked her hair behind her ear, dropping a gentle kiss on the top of her head. "It's just us."

Silently, she offered him the glass. He took a sip, welcoming the burn of the alcohol as it chased away the chill of fear. If anything happened to Chelsea...

She rubbed her cheek against his chest, letting out a soft breath. "You left the room before I could tell you, but the shelf in the closet broke. In all the mess, I found a necklace Richard gave me. I got a little crazy. But..."

"You're not paranoid if they really are out to get you?" Jeremy said.

She pulled away, setting down the glass on the counter, and turned to face him directly. "Look, Jeremy, I know you have reasonable explanations for all the odd stuff that's been happening, like guests using our laptops, or your junk overloading the closet shelf, or me forgetting where I left something. But I really think something's going on. It's like that quote from *Goldfinger*: 'Once is happenstance. Twice is coincidence. The third time, it's enemy action.'"

After taking a moment to appreciate his good fortune in having a hot fiancée who could also quote *Goldfinger,* Jeremy said, "While I'm pretty set on the idea that Richard is locked away and couldn't possibly orchestrate this without the cartel—who are no longer his friends anyway—I agree that we need to be better protected. I'm going to install a security system with a live video feed. We'll be able to keep track of every person coming in and out of here. I'll make you feel safe again, Chels, I swear it."

She buried her face in his chest and nodded, and he curled his hand around the back of her head. "Did you get the stuff on the list?"

He knew what she was doing. Trying to focus on the good and not the bad, which was very un-Chelsea like. "Yep. Bowl, floating candles, and stones for the bottom…and all that shit you had me get."

She laughed.

Goal accomplished.

He kissed her forehead again, his mind going a million miles a minute. After he resigned from the DEA, he hadn't returned to headquarters. He'd wanted to keep that part of his life in the past. Now, however, he thought it might be time to pay his old coworkers a visit to make certain he knew everything there was to know about Richard and the cartel. If Chelsea's crazy ex *was* back in their lives, Jeremy would track him down and put an end to his games….

For good.

Chapter 9

FAT SNOWFLAKES FELL from the gray sky with a majestic elegance, floating and drifting before they joined the rest of their fallen comrades on the ground, until I could no longer differentiate one flake from the other. The wind was strong today, making the branches of the trees out front scrape against the windows and the siding. I stood beside the pretty "test" centerpiece Jeremy and I had made together. We'd placed it on the foyer table because Jeremy said it was too nice to waste.

I shivered, hugging myself as I stood in front of the window, watching the driveway for Jeremy's truck, but the pristine white snow remained undisturbed. He'd gone into Bangor to hit up his old DEA office late this morning to see if he could discover anything about Richard. The snow had started earlier than they'd forecasted, and was getting heavier, too.

It was starting to look like I might be spending the night at the inn by myself. I could sleep alone. I'd done it for years and I used to prefer it. Now, though, a night without Jeremy holding me close, kissing my shoulder every once in a while…

God, I was becoming such a sap.

Sometimes, Dad would hang around long enough to give us little lessons in toughening up. O'Kane Lessons, as he called them. It might be as small as taking our favorite toy and breaking it in front of us, or as harsh as telling us our mother abandoned us because we cried too much. Either way, the effect was the same.

If he saw me now?

He'd give me a huge O'Kane Lesson. Only instead of the stuffed bunny or my mother, I'd lose something a hell of a lot more painful. *Jeremy*.

No matter what I had to do, I wouldn't risk losing the guy who never let me down. A truck crept up the driveway and I smiled, but it faded when I realized that, instead of Jeremy's blue F-150, this truck was black and the wrong make. Rubbing my arms, I squinted toward the windshield. If Paul had brought our poor excuse for a father here…

I let out a sigh of relief when he hopped out of the truck, clearly alone. The snow dusted his heavy red and black flannel coat and he hunched forward, against the wind, a gray hat pulled down over his ears. He puffed out a breath in the cold winter air, and walked up to the door, breathing into his gloveless fists. It wasn't locked, so I waited for him to come in.

When Jeremy wasn't home, Paul never bothered with knocking first.

"Hello?" The door opened, and he peeked inside. "Chelsea?"

I stepped forward.

He turned his head my way, grinning easily. "You're alone."

A fact he was very happy about. When Jeremy had re-entered my life, my brother hadn't originally been so hostile. But as time went by, and Jeremy stuck around, Paul's resentment grew. I didn't know how to fix it since my version of conflict resolution involved moving away and living under an assumed name. "Yep."

He closed the door behind him and the snowflakes on his jacket melted into dark spots. "Where's Jeremy? Did he finally realize he doesn't belong with the O'Kanes? Looks like he's run away from this wedding like he did last time."

I stiffened, because though Paul didn't know it, Jeremy ran out on his last bride for me. I'd been madly in love with him and he'd been about to marry the wrong girl. So we did what any rational best friends would do in that situation. We made love the night before his wedding. Then I went down to Miami for eight years. As one does.

"He went to Bangor. Not sure if he'll be making it back tonight or not."

"Well, Dad got released even earlier than expected. We're going to get him right now, before the roads start to close." He shoved his hands in his pockets, casually dropping that bomb like it wouldn't affect me. "Get your shoes and coat. We're already late and we haven't even left yet."

How very like Paul to try to con me into getting in that truck with him. "No."

"Read this." He pulled a folded up piece of paper out of his pocket, handing it to me. I took it out of reflex. "It might change your mind."

I tightened my grip on it. "Is it from him?"

"Yes."

God, if he'd put this effort into being around when I'd been a kid, maybe I wouldn't have turned out the way I had. Maybe I wouldn't be so cynical and close-minded. Maybe it wouldn't be so hard for me to believe that Jeremy could love me. This gesture on his part was too little, too late.

And he had only himself to blame.

Because of him, I'd learned how to spot a bullshitter before I was out of diapers.

I shook my head and handed the note back to Paul. "If you choose to pretend he's this great guy who is coming back to finally be a father, then knock yourself out, but I'm not getting on that roller coaster with you. I've been there, and as fun as it was, I prefer the Tunnel of Love now."

His upper lip curled. "That fed made you boring."

"No. He made me normal."

"Like I said." He made a whistling sound and rocked back on his heels. "Boring."

I opened the front door, and cold wind blasted us in the face. I forced myself not to shiver. I couldn't afford to show weakness right now. Not when my brother was staring me down. "I have wedding invitations to address, so if you don't mind…"

"Jesus," he muttered, eyeing the centerpiece. "He really did soften you, didn't he? What would Dad say if he saw you now?"

"I don't give a shit about what he'd say."

I loved my brother and he loved me, but we would *never* agree about our father. I used to be more tolerant of my father's shortcomings, but when Dad betrayed me that last time, I was done. It had been an O'Kane Lesson I never forgot. Paul hadn't gotten his final lesson yet. Dad would fix that now that he was out. It was only inevitable he'd break Paul, too.

It sucked, but it was what it was. There was no changing history or who my crappy parents were, but I could control the future and I would choose to not be a part of my father's life. Just like he'd chosen not to be in mine. "You want to pick him up? Go get him. But I'm not going. And nothing you say will change that."

He stared me down, but when it became clear I wasn't budging, he shook his head and walked past me. "You're gonna regret this. You're turning your back on family, and for what?"

"For *me*." I touched my chest. "And before you even start pointing the finger at my fiancé, he made it very clear he'd be fine with Dad around, if that was what I wanted. This is *my* choice."

Paul snorted. "Once a liar, always a liar. Guess it's true, what they say."

I knew better, but I couldn't resist asking, "What's true?"

"That all girls marry men like their fathers."

I stiffened. "Jeremy is nothing like Dad."

"Tell yourself that, if it helps you sleep at night. But to me, it sounds like he's lying to you." He shrugged and turned to face me, standing on the porch with his hands casually shoved into his jacket pockets. "I'll tell Dad you said hi."

"Don't bother."

Smiling sweetly, I slammed the door in his cocky face and locked it. Even though I tried my best to not let his words bother me, Paul won that round. I kept telling myself that Jeremy wasn't like Dad. He was a good guy. Too good for me.

But that led me to another thought....

What if Jeremy realized he was making a mistake marrying me? What if he ran, or, even worse, slept with someone else the night before we said our vows, like he had when he was supposed to marry Mary? Last time, I'd been the girl who ruined the wedding. This time, I'd be the one left crying at the altar. Maybe that's what really bothered me. After all, everyone knew....

Karma was a total bitch.

Chapter 10

BEING BACK AT his old office was weird as hell. Jeremy glanced out the window, frowning at the heavy snowfall. He'd better get moving soon, or he'd be stuck muddling through messy unplowed roads. His job here was done anyway. He'd spoken to his buddy who was in charge of the Miami case now that Jeremy was gone, and according to him, Richard was still locked away safe and sound in solitary confinement. He couldn't be in contact with any cartel members, which meant the likelihood of him being able to mastermind this latest drama was pretty damn small.

That intel brought Jeremy right back to ground zero, but that was okay. He'd rather be stuck at zero than discover that Richard was back and going after Chelsea yet again.

Agent Walker, a former colleague of his, came up with a red-haired man at his side. "Holland! You're back! I knew you couldn't stay away for long."

Jeremy laughed. "Nope, not back. Just visiting."

"Ah." Walker frowned. "That's too bad."

"Sorry. Still living the civilian life quite happily." He eyed the other man and held his hand out. "Hi. Jeremy Holland."

"Scott Donahue." The man closed his hand over Jeremy's and shook.

"New recruit?" Jeremy asked.

Walker laughed and scratched his balding head. "No."

"I'm from Boston, just in town for some training." The man shifted his weight to his other foot, and gave Jeremy a grin. It was charming. Too charming. Jeremy didn't buy into it. "Then back home I go."

Walker nodded. "He's undercover in the city. He's in pretty deep with a gang down there called Steel Row. Vicious stuff."

"South side of Boston, actually," Scotty clarified, smiling.

Jeremy nodded. "I was undercover, too, before I got out."

"Fell in love with his assignment," Walker said with a hint of disapproval in his tone. "You ever have that happen before, Donahue?"

Agent Donahue laughed. "Nah. I'm not a big believer in love."

"Good. Me, either. Well, off we go," Walker said, smiling one last time. "I'll show you where your training officer's desk is."

After the men left, Jeremy's phone vibrated, so he slid the lock screen and opened the text from Chelsea. Paul stopped by. Tried to get me to go pick up Dad. I got rid of him. All in all, a productive day. How's yours going?

He smiled at the dry sarcasm he could hear, even in the

text. Good. Richard is still in solitary and isn't in Maine torturing us, so there's that.

Thank God.

He tapped his finger on the desk. On the surface, this investigation looked closed. All the "events" could be excused as sheer coincidence. Not sure who else would gain something from messing with you. Maybe it's a false alarm and we're worrying about nothing?

Her response was immediate. My gut says otherwise.

All right. I'll try to see if the DEA has any leads on someone who might be trafficking drugs in Hudson. Not sure which direction to go next, but I'll figure it out.

Actually, that was a lie. He'd just lied to his fiancée.

Jeremy knew where the investigation should go next, and that was the problem. The most logical choice at this point was to go after her father. He gets an early parole, and shit immediately starts to go wrong? It was a coincidence Jeremy couldn't ignore, as much as he *wanted* to. If it was her father messing around their inn, Chelsea would be devastated.

She liked to pretend she didn't care about the man or what he did, but Jeremy saw through that act for what it was. She still cared. His phone buzzed with her reply as his former superior approached him.

"Shit," he muttered under his breath. He slipped the phone in his pocket. "Agent Thomas. Thank you for letting me stop by and visit everyone. I appreciate it."

"We both know you weren't visiting, so cut the crap, Holland."

Jeremy winced. "Thank you for letting me do a little bit of poking around, then."

"You won't be thanking me soon," he said, leaning against the edge of the desk. "Miller said you're still with the O'Kane girl?"

His chest tightened, and that metaphorical anchor that he carried all the damn time got a little heavier. "Yeah. We're getting married soon. Why?"

"If you're marrying into that family?" His former boss twisted his lips. "Then you're coming to dinner with me. We need to talk."

Chapter 11

THE WOOD FLOOR was cold against my ankles and the fire crackled in the fireplace, adding a warmth to the air that Mother Nature was doing her best to freeze. I readjusted myself on the pillow I'd placed on the floor between the coffee table and the couch. Then I rolled my neck in a circular motion until it cracked. Leaning back against the couch, I let out a long sigh as I dropped the calligraphy pen I'd been holding in between my aching fingers onto the table. It rolled off.

I let it.

I had worked my ass off at perfecting the calligraphy and I studied the results with a critical eye. I noticed the *l* was slightly crooked, so I picked up the envelope, ripped it in half, and then tossed it with the other messed-up ones on the floor. I'd been hunched over for the last hour, addressing wedding invitations while I waited to hear the familiar sound of tires crunching over snow and gravel to mark Jeremy's return. The sun had descended hours ago, but the snowfall showed no signs of slowing down. The later it got, the more worried I became about Jeremy trying to make it home. The roads in Maine could be treacherous in icy weather.

Rolling to my bare feet, I stepped over the pile of discarded envelopes and padded up to the window to push the blinds aside. I always closed them as soon as the sun went down. Even if Richard wasn't out there plotting against me, *someone* was, and they didn't need a good view of where I was and what I was doing. Out in the landscape of the property, shadows played with other shadows.

I spotted a long-haired stray cat leaving tiny little paw prints in the snow. I had started putting food out for it the first time I saw it, but it never let me near enough to bring it inside. I'd decided to call it Bobby, since it could either be a girl or boy cat. Bobby was as hard to get close to as I was.

Maybe that's why I liked that furry creature.

The old sycamore tree by the driveway bent and swayed in the wind and a hard pebble of ice hit the window. That's when my phone rang. I jumped back, dropping the blinds, and pressed a hand to my racing heart. Shaking my head at myself, I crossed the room to my ringing phone and muttered, "You're getting weak, O'Kane."

His name flashed across the screen, along with a picture of Jeremy kissing my cheek. I picked the phone up with trembling hands. Safety was something I'd come to prize over the years and Jeremy was my safe place. When he was with me, I knew I could always trust him to watch my back. We could protect each other.

If that made me weak, then so be it. I'd be weak for him.

"Thank God. Where are you? Are you almost home?"

"No, I'm still in Bangor," he said, his voice low. "I went out for dinner with my old supervisor and lost track of time. Are you doing okay down there?"

I swallowed and forced a smile even though he couldn't see me. He knew me well enough to see through my act if I didn't give it my all. If he realized how freaked out I was, he would do everything in his power to get home, no matter how dangerous it would be. "Of course. I've been addressing wedding invitations, but my hand hurts, so I took a break. I've become quite the master at calligraphy, if I do say so myself. You should see the curves of my—"

"I'm very well acquainted with your curves," he cut in.

A laugh escaped me. God, I loved him. *Jeremy.*

"Sorry, you walked me right into that one," he said, chuckling. "In all seriousness, though, I'm sorry I'm not there to help you."

"That's okay, you have awful handwriting." It was true. Jeremy's handwriting was worse than doctor scribble. When we were kids, I used to be the only one who could read it. "Besides, you're doing more important things. Find out anything?"

"Not really. Is your dad a free man now?"

I frowned. "I think so."

"Look, I just got back to my truck and the roads are pretty nasty up here. Do you mind if I spend the night chasing a lead? Then I can head home at dawn after the roads are plowed."

Chasing a lead. God, he sounded like such a *cop* when he said stuff like that. I fought an instinctive shiver. As an assistant DA in Miami, I'd spent a lot of time around law enforcement, but when I reclaimed the O'Kane last name, I guess I had fallen back into old habits. "I'll be fine. You know me."

He hesitated. "Chels…"

"I'm fine. I'll keep working on these invitations and then I'll crash. Wake me up with a kiss when you come home." I smiled again. "Make it a good one."

"You know I will," he promised. "Lock all the windows and doors."

"*Pssh.* Who you kidding? I did that hours ago."

He chuckled and the sound was impossibly sexy. I shivered for a different reason this time. "Of course you did. Love you, Chels."

"Love you, too."

We hung up, and I stared at the picture of us for a few seconds before I clicked my phone off with a huff. The hell if I was going to sit here moping because my man wasn't home. That wasn't me. I was strong and independent, and I could take care of myself with my trusty bat at my side. Another piece of ice hit the window. Rubbing the goose bumps off my arms, I resolved to get back to work on those invitations.

I walked to the fireplace and bent down to grab another log.

The second I did, I heard *it*.

The telltale footboard creak you only ever read about in horror novels. Only this wasn't a book. This was real life. Someone was *behind* me.

I tried to spin with the log clutched in my hand, intending on using it as a weapon against an intruder, but the second I started to move, something closed over my mouth. It was suffocating me. I was pulled back against a hard chest, my movements trapped by my attacker's arms. I fought wildly, but it was useless. My limbs went numb, like they weren't there at all.

The smell from the rag was noxious and burned through my sinuses as tendrils of black snaked over my field of vision. As the world blurred, I swore I saw my father's old truck outside the window. The last thing I heard was the sound of the log of wood hitting the floor as it fell, and a whisper.

"Sleep tight, darling."

Chapter 12

IN THE MOVIES, damsels in distress always wake up looking impossibly fragile or delicate, gazing around blurrily until someone fills them in on what they missed. Not me. No, I roused to consciousness with a loud, "Son of a bitch!"

I probably would've been throwing punches, too, if I hadn't woken up before the rest of my body did. While I waited for the feeling to return to my extremities, I blinked up at the white ceiling. My head was aching like there was a tiny man banging on the inside of my skull with a hammer, and my mouth tasted gross.

The fire had died down, so I had clearly been out for a while.

The blurry face of my father leaned over me, and I stiffened. "Son of a bitch!" I said again, just in case the universe didn't realize how pissed off I was. I tried to swing at him, but my limbs didn't cooperate. *He'd drugged me. Actually drugged me.*

And the father of the year award goes to…

His face went away, and I wondered if my foggy brain was

hallucinating because I was desperate to make sense out of all this.

Why would my dad be here?

It made no sense.

Groaning, I rolled over a little, testing my mobility since my brain was clearly not working. A rag lay next to me, and it looked so nasty that it was no surprise I felt like I'd licked a dirty sock.

I looked down at my body. Thank goodness I was still clothed, and aside from some new bruises that were making themselves known, I was basically unharmed. Whatever my attacker wanted, it hadn't been me.

Surveying the communal living room, which I was using since we had no guests at the moment, I growled a little when I saw that the wedding invitations I'd so carefully addressed had been tossed on the floor like garbage. My new calligraphy pen lay broken, half hidden under the couch. Every cushion and pillow had been dumped on the ground, but from what I could tell from my position on the floor, the rest of the living room looked the same. I'd been knocked out, and then someone…what? Ransacked the inn? What could they possibly be looking for?

Jeremy.

I had to call Jeremy.

When I tried to sit up, the world spun. I flopped back down and rubbed my forehead, blinking against the darkness that was trying to make an encore appearance. I'd take darkness over the image of my dad's face any day. There was a creak of the front door, followed by the sound of footsteps rushing toward me. I immediately thought it was Jeremy, showing up on his white horse to rescue me again, but then I realized how stupid that was.

Unless I'd been out for longer than I guessed, Jeremy wasn't here. The DEA had some high-tech gadgets, but they hadn't employed personal teleporters yet.

"Jesus, Chelsea. It's me. Are you okay?" Paul asked, his voice laced with worry. "Check the house. See if anyone is still here."

"Yeah, sure, I'll get right on that," I said, relief punching me in the gut. It might not be Jeremy kneeling beside me, but this was the next best thing. My big brother. Paul wouldn't let anything else happen to me.

But that was when I realized that he wasn't telling me to check the house—he was telling someone *else* to, and since I'd seen my dad's face when I came to...

God, no. Not now. Not when I was weak.

Paul frowned down at me. "I'm calling Doc Wilson."

Doc Wilson was your typical country doctor, who did everything from treat chicken pox to explain the facts of life to motherless preteen girls. He lived about a mile down the road and had a truck that could probably go off-roading on Mount Everest. Seeing as I was still dealing with the aftereffects of the drug and, to be honest, kinda wanted someone to tell me that everything would be okay, I let Paul call the doc without complaint.

Then I heard footsteps again, and a blanket snapped out and was laid over me. The sudden warmth made me shiver, making me realize how cold I'd been. I glanced up...and there he was.

Dad.

Guess I hadn't imagined him after all.

His hair was grayer than I remembered, and he had more wrinkles on his face. How old was he now? Fifty-five? Sixty-five? God, I had no clue. Maybe that made me a bad daughter, but the truth was, he was lucky I'd even recognized him.

He frowned down at me and his blue eyes narrowed. If he were any other man, I'd think the shadows in his eyes were formed by worry, but Johnny O'Kane could fake whatever emotion he needed to land his mark. It's part of what made him such a good con man.

Besides, Dad didn't do the whole fatherly concern thing. He'd never been around long enough to show any type of concern at all, let alone be a father. "The front door was wide open, and since your man isn't here, we checked to see if you were okay."

"I...no." I closed my eyes, because I didn't like anything about this situation. "Get out."

"I will." He pressed his mouth into a thin line. "Once you can stand up and kick me out yourself. Until then, I'm staying right here to make sure you're good."

He shouldn't have issued a challenge. O'Kanes never backed down from a challenge and I wanted him gone. *Now.*

Gritting my teeth, I forced myself to sit up, ignoring the spinning room as I planted my palms on the cold wood floor and waited for things to settle down.

Dad called to Paul, "Not paralyzed. Just drugged." He grabbed the rag, sniffing it carefully and then immediately pulling it away from his nose. "Chloroform. Nasty shit."

I stiffened, because even fresh outta jail, Dad smelled the same. The few memories from my childhood rushed over me, but none of them were welcome. I mean, who could forget the first time I saw him arrested, which happened to be on my fourth birthday? Happy birthday to me.

I rubbed my eyes, forcing my feet to root to the floor as I stood. "I'm up. Get out."

"Soon," he said dismissively, ignoring me just like the good ol' days.

I stumbled to the couch. My phone lay on the floor a few steps away, and I stared at it longingly. Paul followed my line of vision, and handed it to me while he kept talking to the doc on his phone.

Dad watched the hand-off, frowning, probably because Paul had done something kind. Dad didn't believe in helping other people without getting something in return. "Who are you calling?"

I didn't answer, choosing to ignore him. He'd get the point soon enough, and then he'd leave. Just like he always did.

Chapter 13

I SWIPED MY finger across the screen, still pretty shaky, but getting a little bit of strength back now that I was upright on my couch. It was a little after ten o'clock, so I'd been out for a good half hour…maybe less. My brain was still kind of hazy on all the details, but I was pretty sure I had hung up with Jeremy at nine thirty. Maybe. Possibly. Definitely.

Behind me, Paul hung up. "Doc'll be here in thirty minutes." He sat down next to me, resting a hand on my knee. "Are you…did he…touch…?"

"No. I'm fine." I could tell what he was getting at, but I wanted to spare both of us *that* conversation, thank you very much. "He just knocked me out, and then ransacked the place, from what I can tell. I'm going to call Jeremy and fill him in."

Dad leaned on the wall, touching the spot where we'd plastered and painted over the bullet holes in the wall from last year's drive-by. Apparently Dad knew a cleaned crime scene when he saw it. Big shocker there. "This wall got shot up, yeah? The patch job ain't bad. Your man do it?"

"Yes, Jeremy did it. He plastered most of the walls in this place because *he* knows how to fix things. *He* doesn't just leave and let the broken pieces sit as they were."

"It was the landlord's responsibility to fix those window screens, not mine." Typical Dad, always passing the buck. "Raccoons getting in wasn't my fault. 'Sides, not like they had rabies."

"Whatever." I poked my screen, selecting Jeremy's name. "I'd say it was nice seeing you, but that would be a lie. You're not welcome here. Go home."

Paul sat uncharacteristically quiet next to me, frowning at Dad.

Jeremy picked up on the second ring. "Hey, Chels. I changed my mind. I'm almost done here, and the snow looks like it's letting up, so I'm going to hit the road—"

"Someone broke in and knocked me out." No point wasting time with small talk when there was something bigger at play. There were no more what ifs about this situation. Someone was after something. We just had to figure out who…and what. "Paul…and my dad…are here. They saw the inn's front door wide open so they came to check on me."

He let out a long string of curses that would make a nun blush. "I'm coming. Are you okay? Did he hurt you?"

"Just my pride," I mumbled, avoiding both Paul and Dad's eyes. "And they broke my calligraphy pen." I knew it was stupid, but I liked that pen.

Dad frowned. "Calligraphy what?"

"Wedding shit," Paul answered, his voice gruff.

Over the phone, I heard Jeremy's car door bang. "With any luck I can be home in an hour or so. Can you ask Paul to stay with you till I get there?"

I pressed my lips together. Let one guy with a dirty rag take you down, and suddenly you needed to be protected. *Men.* "I don't need Paul to watch me. I can take care of myself."

Paul frowned. "I'll stay," he called out loud enough for Jeremy to hear him.

I shot him a dirty look.

"Thank him for me," Jeremy said.

I smiled sweetly at my traitor brother. "He said to kiss his ass."

"You're welcome," Paul said, rolling his eyes.

"Your dad and Paul were together the whole time?" Jeremy asked.

"Yeah." I locked eyes with Dad. "Supposedly."

I knew what he was thinking, because I was thinking the same thing. Since Richard was still in jail, the next logical suspect was my father.

Jeremy cranked his engine. "It had to be someone who knew I wasn't home. I swear to God, I'll figure out who it was, and I'll put them behind bars if it's the last thing I do."

"I don't want it to be the last thing you do," I said, my heart twisting. "Besides, I'm fine. Just a little shaken up, that's all."

"That's what pisses me off. He scared you. I'll make it better, I swear." He stepped on the gas. "I'm gonna concentrate on driving safely now. I'll check in soon. I love you, Chels."

"I love you, too," I said softly.

When I hung up, Paul made a gagging sound.

My family. Even the good ones are nonsupportive assholes.

"Screw you," I snapped. Then I swung my glare toward my father. "And why are *you* still here?"

"Are you actually marrying a fed?" Dad asked incredulously.

I said nothing. Just frowned.

"What did I tell you two about marriage?"

Paul cleared his throat. "To never do it, even if the score would be life-changing. The money won't be worth the hassle of dealing with the aftermath."

"At least one of you listened," he said, his tone hard.

"Since you never stuck around long enough for me to want to impress you, I mostly tuned you out." I pointed at the door. "Seriously, if you don't leave right now, I'll call the cops."

Dad snorted. "Tell them I said hi."

Paul stood. "Chelsea—"

"It's okay. I'm going. I still have my old truck in the garage, so I can drive myself back to your place." He glanced at me. "Chelsea...you're making a mistake getting hitched to a fed, of all people. Mark my words. It'll only bring you trouble."

I crossed my arms, keeping my face carefully neutral. "Guess I like my men untrustworthy. Maybe it's a leftover trait from my childhood."

"Maybe." He shook his head and headed for the door. "You need better security. Left alone in a big place like this, all the way out here? It's not safe."

Despite his fatherly tone—or his best attempt at one, anyway—I couldn't help but think his words were a threat. Even though he'd probably been with my brother at the time of the attack, I still didn't trust him. It didn't mean he was innocent. I frowned at Paul. "You shouldn't have brought him here. I made it very clear I wanted nothing to do with him."

"So you'd rather we just drove by, left you here alone, drugged on the floor, with the front door wide open?" he asked, lifting a brow. When he did that, he looked like Jeremy. Bet he'd never do it again if I told him that. So I kept quiet. "Dad's right, you know. You need more security."

I didn't mention Jeremy and I were already planning to increase security. Anything I told Paul would immediately get passed along to my dad, and the less he knew about our precautions, the better. I didn't trust him, even if Paul did. "I'm not alone. I have Jeremy."

"Yeah?" Paul asked, crossing his arms. "And where the hell was he tonight while you were getting attacked?"

I gritted my teeth, not answering him, because it was none of his damn business where Jeremy had been....

Or what he'd been doing.

Chapter 14

THE TRUCK SLID on a patch of snow as he pulled up the driveway, and Jeremy tightened his grip on the wheel, cursing under his breath. The snow tires on his truck weren't doing much for him. Besides, it was after midnight and he could scarcely see ten feet in front of him.

He was frustrated. He'd just gotten some upsetting news from his old supervisor and he didn't feel like things were safe at the inn. Most of all, he was 100 percent done with all this bullshit. He needed to protect his woman.

He'd spoken to Chelsea several times over the past two hours. She kept him posted about what the doc said and how her brother continued to hover, but it wasn't enough.

He had to *see* her.

Chels was his life. His heart. His home.

Someone had assaulted his home.

And he'd fucking kill them.

After he held her in his arms.

He parked next to Chelsea's car, opened the truck door,

and raced up the driveway, his heart pounding. The second his foot hit the porch, the front door opened, and there she was. His Chelsea. He did a quick once-over of her, searching for any injuries. *Thank God.* It came up empty, aside from the fear shadowing her eyes. He held his arms open, and she launched herself into them. Jeremy hugged her tight, breathing in her sweet flower scent and closing his eyes for a second. "I'm sorry, Chels."

She nodded against his chest. "It's not your fault."

And, apparently, it's not your father's, either.

He locked eyes with Paul, nodding his thanks once.

The other man nodded back.

"Did he hurt you?"

She shook her head again, fisting his shirt.

Paul stepped forward. "Time for me to ask some questions. Who the hell is messing with my baby sister? What are we going to do to stop him?"

"We?" Jeremy asked slowly.

"Yes. We. You've shown us that you can't handle the job on your own." He crossed his arms. "Look, I still don't like that you lied to her, but it's clear you love her. I can't complain about that...so let's figure out who's after her."

Chelsea let Jeremy go, and turned to face Paul. She glanced at her fiancé once, and he nodded his agreement. It was time to fill Paul in. Maybe he'd be able to give them some inside information. "At first we thought it was Richard, but he was ruled out. Then I thought maybe Dad—"

"It's not Dad," Paul said, his shoulders stiffening. "He might have done some shady things in his past, but he's our father. He wouldn't attack you."

"He would if it benefitted him," Chelsea said, jutting out her chin.

"Are you shitting me right now?"

"We're obviously not going to agree on this. The thing is, he was either in jail or with you today, so clearly he didn't attack me…tonight."

Paul shoved his hands in his pockets and lowered his head. "Okay, so who's doing this?"

"Actually," Jeremy spoke up, "I went into Bangor today and had dinner with my old supervisor, Agent Thomas. He's currently digging into a local crime family. The Sullivans." He eyed Paul's lowered head. "Recognize that name?"

Paul nodded, lifting his head and flexing his jaw. "Yeah, but you already knew that, huh?"

Chelsea shoved her hair out of her face. "Dad used to be buddies with the family, but something went down. After that, we were told if we ever saw a Sullivan attached to a project, to turn the other way."

"That's what Agent Thomas said. There's bad blood reaching back twenty-four years now. The DEA has a theory that one turned on the other during a drug run, but it's never been proven, and we don't know who did what."

Paul frowned. "But why would they suddenly be coming after Chelsea after years of nothing? That makes no sense."

"There are suspicions that your dad took something from the Sullivans before he got locked away and they never found where he hid it. Now that he's out, the Sullivans might be pressing him for it, and won't take no for an answer."

"How dangerous are they?" Chelsea asked slowly.

Jeremy met Paul's gaze, who looked considerably paler than before. "Well, it depends on how you look at it. On a national scale, the Sullivans are the definition of small potatoes, but in Maine, they're major players. Anything organized— prostitution, racketeering, protection, the drug trade—they have a piece of it. Compared to the Sullivans, your dad is a guppy, especially since he's been out of the game for so long. If he doesn't return what he stole, the Sullivans will do whatever it takes to get it back, including…"

Then he turned to look his fiancée directly in the eyes and said, "Using you as leverage."

Chapter 15

THE NEXT MORNING, we left the florist's shop under a heavy cloud of silence. I distracted myself by picking out the flowers—pink valley valentines—for our wedding. That cheered me up for a bit. But as soon as I walked out the door, a cold, hard reality set back in.

My mind was on my dad's beef with the Sullivans again. Since my safety was at stake, I had a feeling Paul would do anything he could to pry Dad for information.

But honestly, he shouldn't bother. Dad wouldn't talk unless he wanted to. Even if his daughter's life was on the line.

There always had to be something in it for him.

"Chelsea," I heard Dad's voice call my name.

I stiffened, turning slowly, and let out a long internal groan. "Dad."

"Jeremy." Dad straightened his knit cap and shrugged inside his winter coat, holding an oil-stained hand out for Jeremy to shake, frowning. "You've grown, son."

Jeremy took his hand, giving him a tight smile. "Ten years will do that to a man."

"Is that how long it's been?" Dad asked, stepping back.

"Ye—"

"Drop the niceties," I said to Dad, tugging Jeremy back to my side. "And tell us what you took from the Sullivans."

Dad closed down. No emotion. No fear. *Nothing.* "I don't know what you're talking about."

"They're coming after me. My inn. Our home." I lifted my chin and grasped Jeremy's hand. "If you ever cared about me, you'll fix this. You'll give them whatever they want."

"I don't know what you're talking about," Dad repeated slowly.

I laughed. "Of course you'd say that. Don't show your cards until you see the size of the pot, right? Only this time, you're gambling with our lives."

"Chelsea…" Dad started, his tone hard as stone.

"Don't. If you refuse to give them what they want—"

"You have no idea what you're asking me to do," he interrupted gruffly.

"I knew it. You did take something."

"No." He clammed up, admitting nothing.

How *typical.*

If Dad was already buried in this mess, and he only *just* got out of jail yesterday, then he needed to stay the hell away from us and our inn. And I refused to let Jeremy get dragged into this dangerous situation for another second.

He shouldn't have to keep risking his life just because he loved me.

Besides, Dad was already out of my life before this happened.

Now he'd stay that way.

I held up a hand. "Fine. You want to be like that? Knock yourself out. I don't care. But if you want to risk your life to run a scam on the Sullivans, then make it crystal clear I'm not in your life. That hurting me won't hurt you a bit. It shouldn't be very hard."

"They won't believe me."

I let out a sarcastic laugh. *Did my father seriously think I'd buy a line like that after the way he'd ignored me when I was growing up?* "Make them believe it. Stay away from us. Don't call. Don't text. Don't stop by unannounced. Ignore us if you pass us in town. Like you used to."

Then I caught Jeremy's hand and we walked away. Jeremy glanced over his shoulder. "Chels—"

"Don't *Chels* me. I'm fine."

As we made our way home in Jeremy's truck, I slowly lost the tension in my shoulders, while he stayed silent the whole time. He was good at that. At knowing when to shut up and when to press me. When I let out a sigh, Jeremy side-eyed me as he navigated down the icy road that led to our inn. "Are you okay?" he said quietly.

"Yes. You?"

"I'm happy if you're happy. But you don't have to—"

Jeremy cut off midsentence when his phone rang over the Bluetooth system. "Shit, hold on. I need to take this." He pressed the Talk button on his steering wheel. "Charlie! My man."

"Hey, Jer." A man who was apparently named Charlie said jovially. "What's up?"

I mouthed *Jer* at Jeremy, and he rolled his eyes before saying, "Still own that security company?"

"Best in the business. Why? You need something?"

Jeremy rubbed the back of his neck. "I need the highest rated security system you have for residences. Cameras. Alarms. Full surveillance. You name it, I want it. And I'll pay cash and a bonus if you start tomorrow."

I leaned back in the truck seat.

Silence, and then, "Where?"

"My home," he said, sliding the truck back into park. "The McCullagh Inn."

"I'll be there at nine thirty in the morning."

They hung up and Jeremy glanced at me. "Well, now we've taken one precaution against the Sullivans."

"We need more." I took a deep breath. "We need to make it clear we are not associated with my father in any way, shape, or form."

Jeremy tightened his grip on the wheel. "You don't have to separate yourself from him like that."

"But I *want* to." I shook my head. "He's not worth the trouble."

Jeremy remained silent, staring straight ahead stonily. I could tell he was worried I might regret my decision, but he was wrong. I had no room in my life for Johnny O'Kane. Besides, it wasn't like I was missing out on anything. All I needed was Paul, the inn, and, most importantly, Jeremy.

They were all I needed to be happy.

Chapter 16

THE NEXT MORNING, as we lay in bed together, the morning sun crept through the edges of the blinds, brightening the otherwise dark room. I was in the middle of a crazy, emotional whirlwind of crap, and the only thing getting me through this disaster called life was the man who held me in his arms like I was the greatest treasure on earth. Sometimes I actually believed I was.

God, that was corny, especially for a girl like me.

But that didn't make it any less true.

Jeremy played with my hair and sighed, slowly turning those bright-green eyes my way, pulling me back into the present. His brown hair was messy, sticking up in places it shouldn't. "Let's make this cake choice, so I have time to stop by the county clerk's office on my way home from the bakery. That way, I can see what's up with that property you want."

I fidgeted with the sheet draped over my chest, suddenly feeling hesitant about the plan I'd come up with. "Do you think purchasing the lot next to ours is a good idea right now, with everything else going on? Or am I nervous for no reason?"

"It's absolutely a good idea. You said it yourself: Once we're having weddings here, we're going to want to put in a pool to make this place the best inn in Maine. Maybe a hot tub, too." He smiled at me, and lifted another forkful of delicious cake for me to try. "Open up."

I opened my mouth obediently.

When he'd suggested we lay in bed this morning and munch on our wedding cake samples instead of breakfast, I quickly realized the genius of the suggestion. So I upped the stakes and stripped, slid between the sheets, and entered heaven on Earth.

He slid a fork filled with vanilla cake and buttercream icing in my mouth. I chewed and closed my eyes, moaning slightly. After I swallowed, he leaned in and kissed me, getting a surprised laugh out of me. When he pulled back, I grinned and said, "This one gets my vote."

He tried a bite, too, swallowing with a sexy groan. "I agree."

"Really?" Grinning, I swiped my finger over his lip, wiping away a smear of icing. "You like it better than the chocolate with buttercream?"

"Chocolate is harder to get out of white dresses," he said, sliding the empty plate onto the nightstand.

"Hey! I'm not that much of a clumsy eater, so I don't see why…" I broke off, my jaw dropping. "Oh no. No way. We're not doing the 'cake smashing into each other's faces' thing."

He laughed and rolled me underneath him, pinning my arms on either side of my head. "Oh yes we are."

I shook my head. "Nuh-uh. You'll win. You'll duck out of the way too quickly and I won't even get any on you. No way. Not playing."

He laughed, burying his face in my neck and nibbling on the skin there. "But babe, we have to. It's a traditional wedding ritual, and we want to show our guests that we can provide the whole package, right?"

Groaning, I arched my neck to allow him better access. He dipped lower, nipping the curve of my bare breast. "Damn you, you're right."

"I'd say I would take it easy on you, but we all know how much you hate pity...."

I slapped his bare butt, the sound of skin on skin filling the room. "I hate you."

"No, you don't." He slid down my body, taking a nipple in his mouth. "You love me."

Threading my hands through his hair, I let my eyes close as he dipped lower and lower over my body. Moments like these were the only things that kept me sane right now, especially given my current circumstances.

Being with Jeremy offered me small slices of normalcy in a world full of crazy.

"I especially love when you do that," I said, ending on a groan when he traced his fingers down my body. His mouth closed over me, and he worshipped my body tenderly, with only a hint of desperation tinging the otherwise romantic moment. When we finished, he rose on his elbows, studying me closely. His stubble was dark along his perfect jaw, and his perfect kissable lips, and his perfect skin. Everything about him was perfection, and I was only…me.

It still didn't make any sense.

Him loving me.

"We're going to be okay, Chels."

"I know." I bit down on my lower lip. "But—"

The doorbell rang, cutting me off. My heart immediately leapt, and I hated that my first reaction to someone on my porch was now fear. I'd been here before. I didn't want to be back.

"Shit, I forgot." Jeremy cursed, jumping out of bed and heading for the dresser. "It must be nine thirty."

Guess that meant the security company was here.

I followed Jeremy out of bed, pulling a shirt over my head. I checked the clock as I stepped into my leggings and covered a yawn with my hand.

He smoothed his hair, and shot me a smile. "You should get some rest, I'll deal with them."

I blinked, because sleep sounded excellent. Last night I'd been too worried to sleep. Yawning, I let Jeremy lead me to the bed. He pulled the covers back, and gently pushed me down. I cooperated, lying on my side. I couldn't keep my eyes open anymore, with all that yummy cake filling my belly, so making him happy by letting him care for me was only a nice bonus. I was a giver like that.

"Once Charlie's done," he said, "this place will be locked up tighter than Fort Knox. No one will get in unless we want them to, and no one will ever hurt you again."

I curled my arm under my pillow and tried my best to smile as he tucked me in and kissed my temple. I didn't put much stock in alarm systems, seeing as I'd watched my dad's crew break through basically every kind of security in existence. "And if they somehow get in anyway?"

"Then they'll answer to me," he said with steely determination, opening the gun safe by the bed, and sliding his Glock into position on his hip. I hadn't even seen him put his holster on. "They'll find out that I'm not so easy to get past. Either way, you'll be safe."

After he left the room to let Charlie in, I stared at the gun safe, shivering slightly even though he'd covered me up. "But who will keep you safe?" I asked the empty room, my voice a mere whisper. There was only one answer.

Me.

Chapter 17

EVEN THOUGH JEREMY had planned to stop by the county clerk's office three days ago, life had gotten in the way, and he was just getting around to it now. Since Chelsea had ordered her father to stay away from them, and they'd put up the new security system, things had been quiet. No break-ins. No papers missing or moved. No unlocked doors that should've been locked.

All in all, life had been peaceful.

Some people might say whoever had broken into their inn had found what they were looking for. That the danger was gone. Some people might let their guard down, start to make careless mistakes. But Jeremy Holland wasn't just anyone. And he didn't like mistakes.

According to his buddy at the DEA, one of the Sullivans had cornered Chelsea's father at his favorite bar last night and had issued an ultimatum. He had a week to give them back what he stole or they'd start killing off everyone he loved.

Which was ironic, because according to Chelsea, the only person Johnny O'Kane truly loved was himself.

But the Sullivans would assume he loved his kids.

No one was safe.

Jeremy pulled into the county clerk's office and parked in the shade. Only sheer willpower kept him from turning left instead, so he could head out to the Sullivan mansion and confront them. He didn't like being in this holding pattern, waiting for something to happen. He preferred to go after his problems.

This didn't feel right. *Waiting.*

But Jeremy wasn't an agent anymore, and he was reduced to begging for updates from his buddies who were on the Sullivan-O'Kane case. Gritting his teeth, he pulled up next to a light-colored truck. His phone buzzed, and he checked it. It was a text from Chelsea. Don't forget to find out if there are any liens on the property. It'll slow things down too much if there are.

Yes, dear, he texted back.

Shoving his phone away, he went into the office, waited around while Mrs. Mathers dug up the necessary paperwork about the land next to the inn for their pool. Jeremy foresaw years of fishing out raccoons and chasing away deer who wanted a swim, but whatever Chelsea wanted, he'd make happen. Even if it meant watching Mrs. Mathers hunt and peck on a keyboard for a good half hour.

She'd looked like she was a hundred back when he'd been in high school and he'd seen her hobbling down the sidewalks of Main Street, and now she looked twice that age. It was a miracle she was walking....

Let alone working.

"Ahh, yes," she mumbled, head bent as she clicked on the mouse. "Here it is."

He leaned on the counter and glanced out the window. After this, he was off to meet Chelsea at the florist to discuss the boutonnieres for the wedding. The things he did for that woman he loved.

As he watched, two men walked by his truck too slowly for comfort. He didn't recognize them. They wore expensive clothes and shiny black loafers that looked out of place in Hudson, which was a small town filled with flannel and construction boots. They stopped behind his truck, partially obscured by the cab, with their heads lowered as they texted on their phones.

"Thank you, Mrs. Mathers," he said distractedly, watching the two men. "Is there a lien on the property?"

"I don't believe so...there are a few notes on here, but you'll have to reference the codes and see what they're about yourself." She frowned. "I'll print everything out for you and give you an application to purchase the property in case you decide you want it. There've been a few offers already, but no acceptances. The owner is being picky about who he'll sell it to, from what I can see."

"Excellent. I'll be sure to make him an offer he can't refuse." The two men moved past his truck, disappearing around the corner of Main and Fourth Street, and Jeremy relaxed slightly. By the time Mrs. Mathers pulled up all the necessary forms and paperwork, it was close to an hour later. As he approached his truck, the hairs on the back of his neck rose. He glanced around, trying to locate what was making him uneasy, but the street was empty, minus the regulars hanging around the coffee shop. They were mostly moms, chugging back coffee while their kids were in school. He turned and looked the other way, and stiffened when he saw the black sedan parked a few feet away. If he wasn't mistaken...

The two men sitting inside it were the same ones who'd checked out his truck.

Looks like a fight had come to him.

Grinning, he walked toward them, heart pumping, because he'd finally gotten close enough to shake down some assholes, and maybe get some answers. Yet when he approached the car, the passenger nudged the driver, and they peeled away from the corner, pulling an illegal U-turn. Jeremy watched them go, fists clenched, knowing he couldn't catch them.

Chapter 18

I SMILED NERVOUSLY at the woman sitting across from me. She had blond hair, brown eyes, and a smile that told me she was as uncomfortable as I was. I knew how to cross-examine someone on the witness stand, but small talk was beyond me. Jeremy and I had a deal. I did the research, found the best person for the job, and he did all the schmoozing. Which is why he should be here, damnit.

After a maintenance issue on the upstairs bathroom pipes cropped up, we canceled our original plans of going to a wedding show in Bangor and instead moved up our appointment with the photographer. However, the repairs on the pipes were taking longer than expected so I was left to, ugh, chat with this poor woman alone.

Judging from the look on the other woman's face, she could tell I wasn't up for this. I forced my smile to go a little wider, and rested an elbow on my crossed legs. "So...Ms. Rollins—"

"Please, call me Hannah," she interrupted, smiling.

"Okay. Hannah." I smiled back. "So...you're a photographer."

Hannah looked confused at my Captain Obvious question, but nodded enthusiastically anyway. "I am. I've been photographing weddings for three years now, and I specialize in outdoor weddings hosted at a smaller venue, like this one."

"*Mmmhmm.* Good. Excellent." I scribbled down what was supposed to be notes for Jeremy, but ended up being a drawing of a stick figure holding a camera. I stopped drawing, studying her. She looked like a shrewd woman who wouldn't take an opportunity to advance her own career for granted, so maybe I needed to be more straightforward. "Do you have much experience with shooting with a more...*commercial* frame of mind?"

"Commercial? Yes, of course." Hannah hesitated, her face still a mask of polite uncertainty. "This is for a wedding, though, right?"

I smiled. "Yes. But..."

"Would it help for you to know that I have tons of experience with advertising, too?" She pushed a book across the table toward me with two perfectly manicured fingers. I stared at it, but didn't pick it up. Instead, I slid my chipped, barely polished fingers under my thighs. She was so composed. So perfect. And so *pretty.* "You'll see the shots I've taken at some weddings in here."

"But have you ever shot a wedding that was as much an ad as it was a momentous occasion?" I asked, keeping my tone perfectly level.

She blinked at me. "Um...no. What exactly do you mean?"

"We're the owners here, and while we're getting married because we love each other, obviously, we also want to make sure that this wedding shows everyone how wonderful a venue this would be for their own special occasions. Therefore, we're going to need good shots for the brochures. It would, in theory, provide a platform for both of us."

She dropped the mask, allowing that shrewdness to surface, and leaned closer. "Fantastic idea. Go on."

Her reply upped my excitement factor. "As you said, this is a smaller venue, so we want to be in a position where we can provide everything a bride would need for her dream wedding," I said in a rush. "So we're looking into contracting with local suppliers and craftsmen. If your photos are amazing and we decide to use them in our brochure, you could certainly be our top recommended photographer."

Her eyes lit with excitement. "Do you have your dress yet?"

"What?" I'd just handed this woman a major career opportunity and she was, what, spot-checking my wedding planning? Guess I hadn't found my girl in Hannah after all. "No. I have an appointment—"

"What dress size are you?"

I instinctively answered with my size, caught off-guard by her intrusive question, and she grinned like I'd just handed her a Pulitzer.

"Perfect. You can wear my sister's dress."

"I can find my own dress, but thank you." I stood, forcing a tight smile. This interview was over. "Thank you for—"

"No, you need to wear hers, and your fiancé will need a tux, and flowers. And...oh! A few guests for the background, too!"

I eyed her nervously. "Thank you for coming, Ms. Rollins."

"No, wait, I'm sorry. I'm not being clear. If you want to do this right, we need to stage the shots ahead of time. We could do it out back, where you're planning to have your own wedding, and wait for the best lighting to take the shots for the advertisement. Anything can happen on your wedding day, so it's best to take these kind of shots in a controlled environment. I'll make your inn look so amazing, people will be dying to come here."

Blinking, I stepped closer, finally impressed. "That's brilliant. I—" The fire alarm shrieking cut me off, and I jumped, slapping my hands over my ears. After I recovered from the shock of the loud noise, I bolted toward the stairs. *"Jeremy!"*

"I'm fine," he called out. He went running by the top of the stairs, hair sticking up, shirt damp, sweat rolling down his cheek, fire extinguisher in hand. "Go outside and call 911!"

I didn't hesitate. I grabbed Hannah's hand and my cell as I bolted outside. Smoke pillowed out of the window of the pink bedroom—*my* old bedroom—and I dialed frantically, my fingers shaking, because if my inn burned down...

"911, what's your emergency?"

Hannah glanced over her shoulder, her brow creased with worry.

"There's a fire—" I cut myself off, as Jeremy came through the front door, fire extinguisher still in his hand, waving frantically.

"It's out. It's done. It's over."

I tightened my grip on my iPhone. "Are you sure?"

"Yes." He locked eyes with me, breathing heavily. "It's out."

"Miss?" The dispatcher called out. "Are you in danger?"

"No. I'm not. We had a fire, but my fiancé put it out. We're fine."

After a few more assurances, we hung up.

Jeremy spoke with Hannah, and shook her hand. She walked toward me, smiling at me as she approached, her eyes warm with compassion. "I'll be back next Friday with the dress, if you're still interested in having me. Your fiancé said he can have a tux by then, and I'll see what I can do about getting some friends to come be fake wedding guests."

I nodded distractedly, studying Jeremy. He looked exhausted and pissed off. *Ditto.* "Sounds good. Thank you, Hannah."

She left, and Jeremy turned to me, opening his arms, like he always did. He was always there for me. My rock. I threw myself at him, holding on tight. When I heard that alarm go off, I'd been sure he had been hurt. I'd thought something had gone horribly wrong and he'd caught on fire. God, I don't know. I hadn't exactly been thinking logically in my panicked state. "Jeremy…"

"I know. I'm fine. We're fine. There was hardly any damage.

It looked like a lamp shorted and sparked a flame." He brushed his hand down the back of my head, smoothing my hair. "But…"

"But we both know it wasn't that," I finished for him.

He nodded, kissing my forehead as his grip tightened on me protectively. "Right. We know what this really was, even if we can't prove it."

Yeah. Sabotage. That's what it was but neither of us wanted to say it out loud.

"The security alarm never went off, so I'm going to check the cameras and see what happened."

I winced, because, God, I was an idiot. "I disabled the system so the photographer could come in without knocking. I forgot to reset it."

"Chels…" he said, looking at me with narrow eyes.

"I know." I ran my hands down my face. "It was stupid. I won't do it again."

He nodded, glancing toward the trees near the front of the driveway. "It's all right. Let's go inside before someone else comes along and catches us off guard."

I glanced up at the sky, following him as he caught my hand and urged me along faster. Everything felt wrong, like the sky was falling all around us, and there was no way to stop it, but I knew one surefire way to stave it off.

And I was going to do it.

Chapter 19

AS CHELSEA WALKED down the stairs before him, he watched the gentle sway of her hips. She was so graceful. So strong in the face of a storm. She was like a steel pole in a hurricane, standing upright without bending…and just as damn *stubborn*. "What did you ask Paul to do? Your brother isn't exactly the most levelheaded person in the—"

"It's nothing serious. It's a small, slightly manipulative tactic my father will respond to. He's the kind of man who responds to…to…intimidation, rather than pleas." She kept walking, picking up her speed. She always did that when she didn't want to answer a question, like she could outrun it, or him.

"What did you do?" he asked cautiously. "And is it illegal?"

Glancing over her shoulder at him, she didn't meet his eyes, which unfortunately gave him all the answer he needed. "I just asked him to—"

The front door burst open, and they both froze on the steps as the alarms blared in the inn. Paul stood there, looking up at Chelsea with wide eyes. "Did you *seriously* ask me to hire some thugs to kidnap Dad and isolate and *torture* him until he tells us what the Sullivans want and where to find it?"

Jeremy's jaw dropped. No wonder she didn't want to tell him what crazy plan she'd concocted last night after the latest incident. "Jesus, Chels."

Chelsea marched the rest of the way downstairs and punched in the code that shut the alarms off before the cops were called. "Don't look at me like that. I'm done playing games, and I'm sick of my inn, *literally,* being placed in the line of fire."

"I'm not kidnapping our father!" Paul said with exasperation laced in his voice. "What are we, trapped in an old-time mafia movie? Who the hell kidnaps their own father like that?"

Chelsea pointed at herself. "Me. He refuses to give us answers, so I'm taking a page out of his own book. I'm not asking anymore. You need to do it."

Paul glanced at Jeremy, and they shared a long, commiserating look. "No, we don't. I'll get it out of him eventually. I've been working on him...*legally.*"

She watched them closely, her lips pressed tightly together. "What the hell was that?"

"What was what?" Jeremy asked immediately.

"That look." She gestured between him and her brother. "You guys don't do that."

Paul shrugged. "Guess we do when you're talking crazy."

"Someone set my inn on fire last night, Paul. *Fire*. I'm supposed to be focusing on my wedding, on my new start with Jeremy, and instead, someone is setting fires and attacking me when Jeremy isn't home!" She grabbed Paul's hand and didn't let go. Jeremy saw Paul's face soften at the touch. "I can't play his game anymore. I just can't."

Paul rubbed his face with his free hand, and let out a long, dragged-out sigh. "I can't do this anymore, either. All I want is…"

Chelsea squeezed his hand. "What?"

"All I want is our family back together again. All of us. Happy. Talking." He glanced at Jeremy, his cheeks going a little red. "Like you two are. I want that, too, but with Dad. You know how he is. We'll get it out of him, sooner or later."

"He's not just messing with the inn, Paul. He's gambling with our lives."

"It won't come to that," Paul argued. "Dad's always looked after us, in his own way, and he won't let the Sullivans hurt us. He told me he really wants to be here for the wedding, to walk you down the aisle. To go legit, like you. Give him a chance—"

"If he really wanted a chance, he'd give them what they want." Chelsea crossed her arms. "You're walking me down the aisle, not him."

Paul froze. "What?"

"You heard me." She lifted her chin. "He's not welcome here. So kidnap him or don't. But if he doesn't fix this, and fix it now, I'll never forgive him. And you'll never get your happy family."

Jeremy saw the hurt cross Paul's face, even though he hid it immediately. Clearing his throat, he touched her shoulder. "Chels…"

Just as Paul opened his mouth to say something, a spray of water came down over their heads. It was the damn pipe he'd been working on yesterday when the fire broke out.

Paul shoved his hands in his pockets, water dripping down his forehead and over his nose. "Looks like you have a leak. I'd offer to help, but it appears I've been given an ultimatum involving our father…so I'm afraid I can't stay."

Then, without looking back, he walked out the door. Chelsea slammed it behind him and screamed a few obscenities about fathers and brothers, and pipes and water.

And in his head, Jeremy silently echoed them as he bolted up the stairs.

Chapter 20

THE NEXT MORNING, I sat at the dining room table with heavy eyes and an even heavier heart, watching Jeremy make our coffee. He'd been so supportive through everything. Silent when I needed him to be. Loud when I didn't. Sometimes I couldn't help but wonder what I'd done to deserve him, because the truth was, I *didn't* deserve him. But I had him, and I was keeping him.

Guess I was selfish like that.

I was an O'Kane, after all.

He slid the cup of coffee in front of me, and I caught it, my ring clinking against the cup again. I didn't think I'd ever get used to the thrill that sound gave me. I yawned and watched as he settled in across from me, resting his foot in between mine on the chair. He eyed me, his five o'clock shadow giving him an almost mysterious air. "You okay?" he asked, his voice still a little rough around the edges from sleep.

I nodded, lifting my coffee to my nose and inhaling the vanilla aroma. "Just tired."

"Yeah." He rubbed the back of his neck and shot me a sexy grin. "Me, too. But at least the pipe is fixed."

"Until it's not," I muttered.

"Hey." He covered my knee with his hand under the table, locking eyes with me. "We've faced worse than a few busted pipes and a fire from a lamp. In the face of what we were fighting when we got back together, all of this is pretty damn normal—"

"And being attacked in our own home?" I supplied helpfully. "Is that normal, too? Is that what our normal is going to be? Always being in danger?"

He frowned, remaining silent. "No. It won't always be this way."

"How can you be sure?"

"Because I am," he said, his voice steady. "And if that is our normal, if we're constantly fighting some unknown danger, then so be it. We'll do it together, and we'll win, every damn time."

I swallowed. God, the man was good at inspirational speeches. He'd even made a believer out of me. As I reached for his hand, the phone rang, so I picked up the cordless receiver sitting on the table instead. "The McCullagh Inn, this is Chelsea, how can I help you?"

"Yes, this is Tom Bradford. I'm calling to reschedule my canceled reservation."

I frowned. "I'm sorry, I must've missed your call about needing to cancel. Did you leave a message?"

"No…you left a message for me. Or, rather, a man did. He said there was a fire, and a few burst pipes.…" The man on the other line cleared his throat. "Was he wrong? Is everything okay up there?"

I tightened my grip on the phone. "Everything is fine, Mr. Bradford, and there must have been an error in communication from my employee. There's no need to cancel your reservation at all. The McCullagh Inn is open for business, and your room will be available when you arrive."

Jeremy frowned, watching as I finished with Mr. Bradford. The second I hung up, he leaned across the table. "What the hell was that about?"

"One of our guests got a call from a man saying that his reservation was canceled due to the fire and the busted pipes."

"Seriously?" Jeremy asked. "I didn't call him."

"I know. And I have a strong feeling Henry didn't, either. Our bellboy's a good kid. I think you know exactly what this is."

Jeremy stood stock still and looked me straight in the eyes. "Sabotage," he said.

I stood in agitation, stalking to the kitchen. Ripping my ring off, I placed it on the counter and turned the water on. I couldn't stop these harassments, but I *could* fix the dirty dishes that were overflowing the sink and spilling onto the counter…so I chose to focus on that right now, thank you very much.

He followed me into the kitchen. "What's—?" The ringing

phone cut him off, and he stared at it. "Do you think that'll be another person calling about a cancellation?"

"Definitely." I poured dish soap into the sink. "You take over. I have to wash these, and then I'm going on the wedding website to stay organized. Can you handle the calls? You're better at this stuff anyway."

He nodded, kissed the top of my head, and took charge of the customer service portion of the morning. He said the same thing, over and over again, telling all our future guests that everything was fine here, that their rooms were safe and sound and just waiting for them to arrive. He was better at placating them than I was.

As for me, all I wanted to do was focus on wedding dresses, and flowers, and the happy stuff like that. While I washed the dishes, I mentally scrolled through the A-line dresses I'd looked at. There was a ball gown dress that looked like it belonged in a fairy-tale wedding, and my heart pounded hard in my chest as I remembered the details in the skirt, the beads, and the tulle. My dream dress.

It was so very *girly*. I loved it.

In the back of my head, I could hear Paul snickering at the fancy gown, but it died away pretty quickly. After all, he'd confessed to having a dream, too. He wanted his family back together.

Wanted us to be normal.

Hah. The O'Kanes. Normal. That was something to snicker about.

Jeremy hung up with the last guest, heaving a sigh. "Well, that's done."

I nodded, dropping a fork into the drying rack.

"Chels…" He came up behind me, closing his arms around me and hugging me. I closed my eyes, letting myself lean against him for a second. Just a tiny, little second. "You and me, together, right?"

I couldn't talk, didn't trust myself not to break down in tears, so I did the next best thing. I turned and wrapped my arms around his neck, lifting my face to his. He kissed me without hesitation, knowing what I needed even though I hadn't said a single word. Then again, he was good at that. At knowing what I needed. At loving me. At pretty much *everything*.

Chapter 21

JEREMY PULLED HER against his chest, wishing he could wipe away all the stress in her shoulders, and the fear that turned her eyes a darker shade of blue. If only a kiss could take all that away....he knew it wouldn't, but it might make her forget about her anxiety for a little while. And maybe forgetting for a few minutes would be enough. His lips moved over hers, and he lifted her on the counter, stepping between her legs. He dug his fingers into her soft thighs, then glided them up slowly, toward her core. Her skin was so smooth. So perfect. He slid his fingers under her pajama shorts, tracing her core through her panties.

She gasped and strained to get closer, her still-soapy hands closing on his shoulders and her nails piercing through the fabric of his T-shirt. She tugged, yanking it over his head, only breaking off the kiss long enough to do so. The second it was off, he dropped so his head was between her thighs, and shoved her shorts and panties to the side with two fingers.

Chelsea planted her palms on the counter, arched her

back, and leaned against the cabinet, a short breath escaping her. He ran his tongue over her, closing his eyes as he breathed in her sweet scent. Her hips lifted, silently asking for more, so he did what he always did when she asked him for something....

He damn well gave it to her.

Her hips thrashed with a wild abandon as he rolled his tongue with slow, steady strokes, making them move faster and harder with each soft cry that escaped her lips. She froze, her whole body tensing, and then threw back her head, her hair draped down her arched back, like it would be in an erotic painting. She was a work of art, his Chelsea.

And he'd do anything to preserve her.

He stood, buried his fingers in her long brown hair, and melded his mouth to hers as he stepped closer, back between her thighs again. He shoved his pajama pants down, used two fingers to pull her clothes out of the way again, and thrust inside her with one long stroke. They moaned simultaneously, lips still pressed together, bodies joined, skin on skin.

These moments, the times when they were joined together in the most intimate way possible, still amazed him even after all this time. He hoped that never changed. Wildly, madly, he moved inside her, strumming her body in all the right places guaranteed to send her flying over the edge again. He squeezed her nipples between his fingers, twisting slightly as his hips moved faster and harder and smoother....

She cried out, her body tensing around his, and he let

himself go, seeking that same bliss she'd found. And when he found it, he groaned and dropped his forehead on hers, breathing heavily. His hands flexed on her hips as he came back down from the high the orgasm had sent through him.

She let out a soft laugh, wiggling a little bit, and then groaning when it was too much. He thrust inside her one last time, laughing when she protested and moaned, "You're *killing* me."

"Never. I love you too much to do that," he whispered, kissing her swollen lips as he slowly pulled out of her. "And I'll stop at nothing to make you feel safe in our home again."

She smiled and framed his face with her hands. "I know. But you see, that's what scares me. What if you do something stupid to save me, and I'm not there to save *you?*"

"I can take care of myself."

"So can I," she shot back.

He frowned. "I know, but—" His cell rang from the counter a few feet to the left. He grabbed it, scanning the number. "It's the DEA."

"Why would they be calling you? You're not an agent anymore."

"I don't know. Maybe one of my buddies got a lead on the Sullivans, and they're calling to give me an update." He swiped his finger across the screen. "Hello?"

"Someone is trying to buy the land next to you, and we think it's someone with ties to the Sullivans," Agent Miller, another friend from the force, said without preamble. "Agent

Thomas wants you to come in. I think he's going to ask you to join in the task force as a civilian consultant. I don't know for sure. But he wants you here at ten o'clock."

Jeremy tightened his grip on the phone, his mind going a million miles a minute. Getting in on the task force would be pretty ideal for their current situation. He wouldn't be in the dark anymore, and he'd be able to protect them better from the inside. But that wasn't his life anymore, and he didn't want it to be. It was too dangerous. Too unpredictable.

Besides, Chelsea wouldn't like it.

He glanced at her, and she lifted her brows in question.

Covering the phone, he whispered. "DEA wants me back to work on the Sullivan case."

"Hell, no," she whispered.

"I knew you'd say that," he whispered. Smiling at her reassuringly, he walked a few feet away, leaned against the counter, and took his hand off the speaker. "Thanks, but no thanks, Miller. I'm not DEA anymore. I run an inn, and I'm perfectly content with that. This is a case you're going to have to solve without me."

Chapter 22

THREE HOURS LATER, I was frantically tearing everything out of the last drawer in the kitchen, tossing all the dishcloths over my shoulder. They landed on the floor next to the pots and pans. I reached the bottom of the drawer and mumbled, "No, no, no. It *has* to be here."

Dropping to my knees, I dug through the mess, looking for the glint of reflection off the lights overhead that would end this torment. My heart was beating faster, but it didn't get me any closer to success. *"Come on."*

The kitchen door opened, and Jeremy stood there, staring at me with wide eyes. He'd been getting fitted for a tuxedo in Bangor. "What. The. Hell?"

"I can't find it," I said in a rush, shoving a big stock pan to the side and crawling on my hands and knees to the next one. "It has to be here somewhere. Not even he would stoop that low."

"Who?" He fell to his knees at my side. "And what?"

"My *ring*." I pushed a pink dishcloth to the side. "I looked at the security footage, and someone bypassed the alarm. He was wearing a hoodie, but the jawline…it looked like Dad."

"Wait." He narrowed his eyes. "What's this about your dad? And your ring?"

"It's *missing,* but Dad wouldn't do that. Not even he is that horrible. Right?"

Jeremy stared at me, his jaw tight. "Your engagement ring is missing?"

"Yes. I took it off to wash the dishes, and after you left, I saw it on the counter, but left it there because I wanted to shower before putting it back on. I went upstairs, and then when I came down to put it back on, it was gone." I crawled toward the sink, my heart pounding harder. "It was there. It wasn't missing. *It was there.*"

Jeremy rested a hand on my shoulder. "Chels? It's gone."

"No." As the horror sunk in, tears filled my eyes. "It can't be gone. He wouldn't do that. He's an ass, but not that much of an ass. Right?"

He said nothing. There was nothing to say because we both knew he would…and he probably did. The footage didn't lie. That jawline was all too familiar to be ignored.

"Why did he do it?" I demanded.

Jeremy frowned and cupped my face, leaning in and kissing my forehead. "Maybe we need to ask him. Maybe we were wrong about the Sullivans, and it's been your dad all along. I don't know, but we need to ask him point-blank what he's up to."

I nodded, knowing he was right.

Maybe we were too quick to take him off the suspect list. It was time to track down the monster hiding under my bed, and confront it head-on with a sword. "It has to be me. Not you. If a fed is involved in the questioning, he'll clam up out of principle, just like last time."

He nodded after way too much hesitation. "Fine. But I'll be down the road on standby, in case he tries anything dangerous."

I wanted to tell him that my dad wouldn't hurt me, that he wouldn't go that far, but I wasn't sure if that was true, and since I'd sworn to be honest to him at all costs…

I said nothing at all.

Chapter 23

THE NEXT DAY, I stared across the coffee table at my father.

It was the only thing separating us. He sat next to Paul and was lounging on the couch with an ankle thrown over his thigh, looking like he didn't have a single worry coloring his life. I had one giant one—and he was on my couch right now, with his cocky smirk and all.

My problem was wearing a gray sweatshirt, an old pair of jeans, and stained sneakers. Paul mirrored his look with a hoodie, Chucks, and ripped jeans. I couldn't handle how similar they looked right now. They wore identical frowns and furrowed brows, and had the same hard jaw and cocky attitude. Like father, like son, I guess.

Jeremy was at the local caterer's, finalizing the payment for our wedding menu, and he had no clue that I had invited my dad and Paul over. I'd pretended to have a headache and stayed behind.

"This needs to stop." I leaned back in the loveseat, tapping my fingers on my thigh.

Dad frowned, glanced at Paul, and said, "What needs to stop? Can you please be a little more specific?"

"Stop ruining my business. I don't know what your endgame is here, but it's a game you're going to lose."

"I don't know what you're talking about," my father said. He seemed sincere but sincerity was something he'd been able to fake before he learned to walk.

"You stole something from the Sullivans. They want it back. And as a result, they've been sabotaging the inn. That's bad enough." I held my bare ring finger up. "But stealing from your own daughter? That is incredibly low, even for you."

"Your ring is missing," he said flatly.

It wasn't a question, but I answered anyway. "Yes."

"Shit," he growled.

I glanced at Paul, not buying his surprised act. Maybe now he'd see why his dream was never going to come true. "Are you in on this? Are you helping him ruin everything I built?"

"*No.*" He locked eyes with me. "I'd never do that to you, Chelsea."

I stared at him for another second, then nodded slowly. "Okay."

"I didn't take your ring. It had to be the Sullivans," Dad said.

I barely refrained from rolling my eyes. "Sure."

"Look." Dad leaned forward. "I'll be completely honest, if

that's what you want. I'll tell you everything I can, but I'm not the villain you've made me out to be. I've changed. I want to be a better father to you, to Paul, and later on, a good grandfather to your future kids."

I stared for a while, not sure where he was going with this, and then laughed. "Yeah. Sure you do."

"How come you believe him, but not me?" he snapped, looking like the old dad I knew…and didn't love…again.

"Because I love him," I said simply. "Drop the bullshit, and tell me what's really going on. Why are you sabotaging the inn and where's my ring? Just tell me why you took it, and why you tried to play me. Then leave me alone for good. I will always be an O'Kane, but the O'Kane lifestyle isn't what I want. I've told you this a million times—I want to run my inn, marry Jeremy, and be normal. Can you just let me be normal?"

Dad's frown lines deepened. "I'd never hurt you, or your inn. I was only trying to protect you."

I met Paul's hopeful gaze and for a second, I felt it, too. I hoped that maybe Dad did care and that we could be a real family. But then I remembered the last time I felt like this. I'd been fourteen, and Dad had let me and Paul work a job with him. When we were working together, in the family business, it had finally felt like we were a real unit. Then, once the job got done, Dad handed me all the cash and sent me off by myself to make my way back to the extraction point.

That's when I realized that I only had real value to my father because I had been a minor.

I could take the blame if we were caught and my father could stay out of jail. I'd vowed then that I'd never let Dad use me again.

Snapping into the present, I kept my voice level and said: "Tell me why you took the ring. If you don't, I'm calling the cops. Last chance."

He was silent for so long that I began to think of other contingency plans.

And all I wanted to do in that moment was turn him over to the Sullivans.

"You're right. The Sullivans are after something." His leg was completely relaxed, draped across his knee, so my father maintained his air of casual calm. "I hid something in the wall in your old bedroom and it's something very important to them. I was trying to keep you out of it, but since you renovated everything, I needed access."

I blinked at him. "So the fire, broken pipes, the cancellations, those were all *you*? You've got to be kidding me. If you're willing to go through all that for the Sullivans, I know you took my ring. And I want it back."

Dad dropped the "casual," leaning forward and staring at me directly. "I had nothing to do with your ring. The Sullivans probably took it when I didn't move fast enough. They're showing me that they can get close enough to steal your ring, so they can get close enough to kill you. This is serious. That's how badly they want what I stole."

There was a quiet groan from Paul and I knew the blinders had finally come off.

Dad continued, "We can try to get that ring back, but really, what's the most important thing here? The ring...or your life? Jeremy's life? You decide, Chelsea."

Chapter 24

I SHOOK MY head. "You want me to believe you didn't take my ring? For God's sake, I saw you on the security footage!"

"I don't know how many times I can say the same thing. I didn't take your ring. You must have seen someone else." There was the faintest hint of temper shining through the words and, oddly enough, that convinced me he was telling the truth.

"I'd know your jaw anywhere. And the man in the hoodie on the footage…"

"The man in the hoodie on the footage? As in, you couldn't even see his face?"

"I didn't need to. I know it was you."

He flexed his jaw, but remained silent.

"When I think of how much time you wasted, how much stress you put on me, how you very nearly ruined my *wedding* day…For God's sake, Dad, you chloroformed me!"

Paul shook his head. "He didn't knock you out, Chelsea.

He was with me that night, remember?"

"And you can vouch for him for the entire time?" I snapped out.

"Yes, Officer." Paul frowned. "I can."

Dad snorted. "Look, the only thing I'm guilty of is making a few phone calls. I figured if I could cancel the reservations from some of your guests, I could talk you two into an early honeymoon. When you were gone, I'd come in and get what I needed." He stood, dragging a hand through his hair. "I wasn't lying about wanting to be better. After I fix this thing with the Sullivans, I want to be there for you. I want to be your father."

"You're about a whole lifetime too late for that," I said dryly.

"Chelsea—"

"What did you hide in my home?"

Dad frowned. "You don't need to know. It's better if you don't. Trust me."

"Because that's worked out *great* for me so far."

"I promise, once I get this mess taken care of, I'll go straight. Let me get what I need, and then I'll prove I can change."

Again, that small part buried deep inside me surged up in hope, and I wanted to take out a fork and stab it right in the stupid face. Guys like Dad? They don't change. "No."

Paul stood. "Chelsea—"

"You can have whatever it is you hid in here, but you can't have me, too." Lifting up my chin, I tightened my fists into balls. "And you're not going to be in my kids' life, if I even have them. I won't let you ruin them, like you ruined me."

Dad said nothing.

"Get what you came here for and get out. Out of my inn. Out of my town." I pointed a finger at him, and it trembled. "Out of my life."

He held his hands out, palms up. "Chelsea, please."

"Do we have a deal?"

He shook his head. In a flash, a memory hit me, of Dad begging some cop for more time, because my tenth birthday was the next day and he didn't want to be in jail for another birthday of mine. The cop refused, and I celebrated with Paul and a social worker who hated me. "Chelsea—"

"Do we have a deal?"

After what felt like a million years of silence, he nodded. "Yeah. We have a deal."

I swallowed hard, my throat swollen and aching with bile.

Once he settled with the Sullivans, my quiet little life could resume. I could go back to focusing on marrying Jeremy. Back to running our inn, and keeping any future children as far away from Johnny O'Kane as they could get. "Then let's get to work."

Chapter 25

JEREMY OPENED THE front door, his arms full of free food the caterer had shoved into his arms after he handed her a check and a contract. It had been a hell of a long day and his mind was filled with worry about Chelsea and her father. He wasn't sure if Johnny was the man behind all these attacks, but he'd seen the footage, and that slightly crooked jawline had definitely been his.

A loud crash sounded from somewhere upstairs, and Jeremy dropped the food on the floor without a second's hesitation. Pulling his gun from its holster, he charged up the stairs, his heartbeat pounding like a set of drums.

He rounded the corner, sliding on the hardwood floor with a short exhaled breath, and slid into Chelsea's old room, hands steady on the gun as he pointed it toward—

"What the hell?"

Chelsea, Paul, and their father all stood wearing dust masks. They had tools in hand and the left bedroom wall was in pieces. Plaster dust filled the air. Jeremy covered his face, backing up as a new puff of the white powder exploded in the air after Chelsea slammed the hammer into the wall again. She fished around in the new hole and let out a triumphant cry as she pulled out a little black book.

Her dad dropped the hammer and snatched it out of her hands, ripping his mask off. "That's my girl. I knew we'd find it!"

Chelsea still had her mask on, so it was hard to see her reaction to her father's praise, but judging by the way her shoulders tensed up, it wasn't a good one.

Paul took his mask off, swiping a dirty forearm across a sweaty forehead, leaving a streak of brown and gray behind. "That's it? That's what you went to all this trouble for? A book?"

Johnny nodded. "It is." He tucked it away in his pocket, and grinned. "It'll all be over, now that I have this again."

Chelsea removed her mask, shaking her hair out of her face. "So what's in it?"

"It's better you don't know."

She pressed her lips into a thin line. "You're going to give it to them, right? So they leave us alone? At this point, don't worry about the ring if you can't get it back. Just make sure they stay away."

"I'll take care of it. All of it." He rested a hand on her shoulder, and Chelsea stared down at it with narrow eyes. "You have my word."

She shook off his hold. "Because *that's* so valuable."

"I—"

"Guys?" Paul said, his gaze locked on Jeremy. He'd been so busy watching the tension between Chelsea and her father that he'd forgotten all about Paul. "We have company."

Chelsea and Johnny turned slowly.

Johnny paled. "Shit. It's the fed."

"No. It's my *fiancé*."

Her father gestured at him. "But—"

"Can someone tell me what the hell is going on here?" Jeremy asked, trying his best to keep his voice level, but failing. "What's in that book?"

"No," Johnny said. "Piss off."

"Don't talk to Jeremy like that," Chelsea snapped. Turning to Jeremy, she said, "The book is what he stole from the Sullivans. He's going to give it back so they leave us *alone*."

"But what's in the book?" Jeremy persisted. If it contained critical information, then he couldn't let them walk away with it. He should give it to Agent Thomas. "Why do you need it?"

"It doesn't matter," Chelsea said, locking gazes with him. "He's leaving, and he's giving it back to them, and then he's never coming back to Hudson. Ever. We'll just pretend he's locked up in jail again. Right, Dad?"

Her father hesitated, but then nodded. "I'll keep my promise."

"Then go."

Jeremy stepped forward. "But—"

"Go," Chelsea said to her father.

Johnny did as he was told.

Paul followed him silently, but stopped at Jeremy's side. "I tried to warn you, cop, but now you have to pick. The O'Kanes, or your precious law and order."

"Her," Jeremy said, his voice low. "It's always her."

Paul nodded in approval. "Good. Then this never happened."

He left without another word.

Once they were gone, Jeremy gritted his teeth and spun on Chelsea. "If there was information in there that could lead to the Sullivans' arrest, and you let it just *walk* away—"

"You chose me," she said, her quiet voice cutting him off as she twisted her hands in front of her. She looked way too vulnerable for his liking. "I know you love me, but you know my family and how they work. If you're uncomfortable letting this one go, then walk out now. Because no matter how far my dad runs, we *will* be in this situation again. So if you can't handle that…if you can't handle me? Walk away now, while I'm watching. It'll hurt less than if you do it later, when my back's turned."

"Chels." He crossed the room and pulled her into his arms, the anger and frustration inside him deflating into a shriveled balloon. "I'm not going anywhere. I'm not leaving you. I love you, and it's you and me, together. Remember?"

She nodded, and to his horror, tears filled her eyes. Chelsea *never* cried, and hated weakness of any sort. He wasn't sure what the hell to do with this version of her, or what to say. "It's over. He's gone."

When she burst into tears, he did the only thing he could.

He held her until she stopped.

Chapter 26

IT HAD BEEN almost two months since Dad left my life with that mysterious black journal in his hand. Ever since, it had been quiet at the McCullagh Inn. No one bothered us. No one threatened us. Dad had kept true to his word.

He'd left us alone, too. No letters. No quiet pleas for second chances. Turned out, he really could keep a promise.

It was sad that I was surprised by that.

I stumbled forward blindly, cursing under my breath. Jeremy was behind me, his hard chest pressed to my back, with his hand plastered over my eyes so I couldn't see anything. He'd told me he had a surprise for me, since I'd been so busy with the wedding planning, making up for lost time. We were getting married in three days, and I couldn't be happier about that, but through all the plans and excitement, I couldn't shake the feeling that something was missing.

I never got my engagement ring back, and I touched the bare skin on my finger where it should've been. Regardless of who'd taken it, I made my peace with the fact that it was lost forever. Jeremy and I would have to find a time to pick out a new one soon. For now, we were going to go through with the wedding ceremony and only exchange our wedding bands.

But there was something bothering me.

"Okay, almost there." Jeremy's voice was low with nerves. Why was he nervous? What was he up to? "Okay, now, before I take my hand off your eyes, remember that I love you very much."

My heart twisted with dread. "Jeremy—"

"Don't be mad at me, but I know you, and you've been upset ever since he left. So this is my attempt at fixing that, and making sure you have no regrets when you walk down that aisle to me on Saturday afternoon." He lifted his hand, and then said. "That being said, I'll leave you to it."

He practically ran from the room, shutting the door behind us. The sound of him locking the supply room was the last thing I heard before I saw who was with me. Then, God, I wanted to *kill* Jeremy, not *marry* him.

"Oh, hell no."

My father held a hand out. "I didn't make this happen. It was all him. I kept my promise, and I stayed away like you asked. But then he told me you missed me, and…"

Yep. I was definitely going to kill my fiancé. Slowly. Painfully. "He was wrong. I'm not upset. At least, I *wasn't,*" I called out loud enough for Jeremy to hear. I could practically hear his flinch through the door. "Let me out of here right now, Jeremy!"

"In a minute," his muffled voice called through the door, the only thing keeping him alive right now.

"I'm sorry," Dad said quietly. He looked older than the last time I saw him. Like his hair was grayer, his wrinkles were deeper, and he just looked...*resigned*. I tried to ignore that, but ultimately failed. "I'm sorry I didn't tell you the truth, and I'm sorry I didn't get your ring back. They're swearing they didn't take it and I can't prove otherwise."

I wrapped my arms around myself. "It's fine."

"No, it's not. I messed up. Again." He shrugged. "I wanted to make a good impression, I wanted that second chance, but I went about it the wrong way."

"You *had* a second chance," I said, my throat swollen. "And a third, and a fourth, and a fifth—"

He winced. "Okay, I get it. But it's different now. I'm different, and it's because of you."

"Me?" I asked, laughing nervously. "You've got to be kidding me."

"I'm not," he said, putting out his hands in front of him, palms up. "You did it. You took the shitty life I gave you, and you made it something good. You have this inn and a man who loves you very much. Even if the guy's a fed—you're happy. And all of that happened even though you had me for a father. I tried to harden you, to protect you from all the shit life was going to throw your way, but I see now I went about it the wrong way. I always do."

I shook my head. "Dad..."

"Instead of hardening you, I should have fought for you. I should have protected you. I should have risen past my lot in life, like you did. Then maybe I'd be walking my baby girl down the aisle instead of wishing I'd been better all the damn time. I won't ask you for a second chance again, but if I could go back to the day you were born, I'd do every damn thing differently. I'd make you proud this time."

Tears blurred my vision. I hated that, but there was no stopping them. For the first time in my adult life, I had the sense that he was telling me the *truth*. That he actually wanted to do better. To be a good man. People changed, right? I changed. Why couldn't he?

The door opened behind us, and Jeremy stepped in, eyeing me nervously. "Okay. Your minute is up, Johnny. Time to go."

I didn't look at Jeremy, since I couldn't take my eyes off Dad. His shoulders drooped as he nodded. He started for the door.

I watched him go, uncertain about what to do. Jeremy was right. I *had* been upset when my father had been out of my life. Even though I couldn't trust him before, I kept wondering if he'd meant what he said now. If he really wanted to go clean. That uncertainty was killing me.

When it came down to it, I'd rather give Dad a chance to prove me wrong than wonder for the rest of my life if I'd been the one in the wrong. I needed to know. I needed that chance.

And Jeremy had given it to me.

God, I loved him.

"Be here at two on Saturday."

Dad froze, turning slowly, his eyes lit up with something I hadn't seen in them for years: hope. "I can come?"

"Well, I'll need my father to walk me down the aisle."

Joy lit up his face, and he pulled me in for a hug. His smell, that achingly familiar smell, washed over me, and for once, bad memories didn't come with it. I pictured him making me get back on my bike on a spring day when I was seven, even though the only reason he'd taught me was so he'd no longer need to drive me anywhere. When I started pedaling, his hand had been on my back as he helped me propel forward before he let me fly free. I closed my eyes, letting myself enjoy this feeling for a second, the same I'd felt while flying on my bike.

Hope.

Chapter 27

I STOOD AT the end of the aisle in my white dress, the small beads picking up soft light from the overhead lights, reflecting off my skin in a delicate glow. The skirt was made of tulle, and puffed out like a ball gown, and I felt beautiful in it. Dad's arm was tense under my hand, and Jeremy stood at the other end, next to a huge floral centerpiece that matched my bouquet, staring at me with so much love in his eyes that it literally stole my breath away. I always thought that was just a saying, a cliché, but God, it was real. You could literally have your breath taken away, and it was a fricking amazing feeling.

He smiled, and without even realizing it, I smiled back.

"I love you," he mouthed and that's when I saw it, the tear in the corner of his eye.

I winked back at him.

He was still here. He hadn't run away. He loved me. He really loved me.

Paul watched us and rolled his eyes, but he didn't fool me. I saw the happiness on his face. He and Jeremy had reached a truce of sorts, and he was going to help us try to launch our wedding business. Looks like Paul was getting his happy little family after all. Go figure.

Valley valentines lined the aisle on either side and the bright sun cast a romantic glow over the ceremony just as we had hoped. The string quartet quietly strummed as they waited for my cue to begin the wedding march. A cold wind whipped my veil to the side, and a quiet lull of conversation filled the evening air. Several guests held brochures in their hands already, and I smiled. Hannah, the photographer, snapped pictures. We hadn't gotten a single regret in response to our invitations. Even the stray cat, Bobby, showed up and sat to one side, taking in everything.

It was the perfect winter wedding in Maine. In our invitations, we'd asked our guests to bundle up for our short ceremony, and wear their finest underneath. We had cleared the snow and ice to make room for the chairs and the trellis, and brought in some industrial heaters to try to keep the chill off. I wasn't going to wear a coat, no matter how cold it was.

My heart was pounding and the adrenaline would keep me warm…and so would Jeremy.

Dad cleared his throat. "You ready?"

"Oh, yeah." I took a deep breath. "I'm ready."

I linked my arm around Dad's, and then tucked my hand back in my white fur muff. We walked down the red carpet aisle we'd laid out, and with each step that took me closer to the man of my dreams, the man who had owned my heart, I felt more ready than ever. We could take it all on. The fear. The doubt. The pain. The worry. Everything. *Anything*. I could handle it all, as long as I had Jeremy by my side. Dad stopped in front of him, and they did the whole formal hand-off thing, as if it really meant anything anymore.

It was stupid, that hand-off.

But it made me tear up.

Jeremy was now the person who'd take care of me for all my life. And I'd take care of him.

He leaned down and whispered, "You look beautiful, Chels. How did I get so lucky?"

"I ask myself the same thing every day," I whispered back.

He glanced down, taking in the delicate beading on the white neckline, and the soft flare of tulle that puffed out like a princess ball gown. It was so feminine. So dainty. So not me.

I *loved* it.

I smiled and kissed him. I couldn't help myself. He leaned in, pressing a hand at the small of my back, and taking charge of the kiss, like he always did. After an undetermined amount of time, the minister cleared his throat, and we broke apart. Holy crap, I'd forgotten where we were…and what we were *doing*.

"May we continue with the wedding? I haven't gotten to the kissing the bride part yet. That will happen at the end," he said with a slightly disapproving tone.

The crowd behind us laughed, and my cheeks went hot. "Uh…yeah. Sure."

We locked hands and faced the minister. So much happiness filled my heart that it was a miracle it didn't burst into a million pieces right then and there. After we said our vows, the sun set behind us. The torches we'd placed strategically around the venue were lit. Everything, in this moment, was perfect.

We'd placed brochures advertising our wedding venue in a tasteful, handcrafted wooden crate behind the last row of seats on the left. They were next to the wedding programs I'd designed by hand, so people had picked them up on the way into and out of the ceremony. As we headed to the garden for more photographs, I heard people whispering about wanting to secure dates before we booked up. Jeremy and I locked eyes and grinned, tightening our grips on each other. We'd done it, together. We'd pulled off the wedding of the century, and it had been a smashing success.

Even more importantly?

We were getting our happily ever after.

Epilogue

THE MAN STOOD at the window of his penthouse office, frowning down at the city lights below him. From up here, people looked like tiny ants, begging to be squashed beneath his shoe. People, as a general rule, needed a leader. A strong man, and one who wasn't afraid to take charge. It's why so many people believed in God. They needed to believe there was a higher power watching over them, keeping them safe.

People needed someone like him.

His brown hair was swept back to the side and gelled to perfection. His blue eyes were best described as cold and calculating, and he had a dimple in his chin that some people found charming. He never failed to use that false charm to his advantage. He straightened the sleeve of his gray Gucci suit and let out a sigh. Somewhere out there, a handful of miles away, Chelsea O'Kane was getting married, thinking she was free of trouble and worry. Somewhere out there, she was smiling, and happy.

It made him sick.

A soft knock sounded, and he called out, "Come in."

"Sir? You've gotten a package."

He held his hand out. "Give it here, please." After she gave it to him, he smiled at her and said, "Thank you. That will be all."

The second the door shut behind her, he tore the envelope open. Inside was a black book he thought he'd never see again, and a cell phone. He flipped through the pages, making sure it was intact, and then opened the phone, dialing quickly. "Sullivan, I was starting to think you'd never deliver this."

"Of course I would. But here's something you should know," the voice on the other end of the line said. "The wedding went over without a hitch. And word is they bought that land next to the inn."

He tightened his grip on the phone, anger pumping through his veins. Did that damn woman ever fail? Did she know what it felt like to lose something important?

He looked down at the photograph on his desk, the one of the family he'd never met, who didn't even know he existed. "Looks like I'll be making my first trip to Hudson soon. Thank you for your help."

After he hung up, he took the SIM card out of his burner phone and dropped it in a glass of water. He watched it bubble and fizzle, then went behind his desk, opening a drawer. He pulled out the tiny black box, opened it and smiled down at the ring inside it. It was beautiful. A true work of art. Just like its original owner had been.

Snapping it shut, he said out loud to the empty room, "You know what they say. If you want to get the job done the right way, you have to do it yourself. Soon we'll meet, little sister."

READ ON FOR A SPECIAL BONUS
EXCERPT FROM

A Princess in Maine
By Jen McLaughlin

The McCullagh Inn is hosting the event of the century.

Chelsea Holland is used to dealing in secrets, and this
one's proving to be the most exciting one yet: her old
friend Grace is marrying a European prince, and Grace
wants to host the wedding at the McCullagh Inn. But is
Chelsea willing to put herself and her inn in the public
eye—especially after being on the run?

Read the story of love and suspense, coming soon from

HE REACHED FOR the doorknob, but it swung inward before he made contact. Chelsea stood there, practically vibrating with excitement. "Jeremy!" she practically shouted, giving a little hop.

The last time he'd seen her this wired, she'd been working on two hours of sleep, countless cups of coffee, and clutching way too many home renovation books. This time, he knew for a fact she'd gotten more sleep, but the coffee and renovation part…

With his Chels, you never knew.

Fighting back a smile, he said, "What's up?"

"Everything." She smiled at him, grabbed his hand, and tugged him inside the inn without so much as a nod in her brother's direction. "You'll *never* guess what just happened!"

"Hello to you, too, sis," Paul muttered, following them inside despite her lack of greeting.

"I'm guessing you booked us a wedding," Jeremy said.

"Not just *any* wedding," Chelsea continued, reaching out with her free hand to squeeze Paul's arm in greeting but not letting go of Jeremy. "And Grace isn't just marrying any average guy. She's marrying a *prince*. And they want to have the wedding here, no expenses spared, and offered us triple our normal—"

"Wait." He held a hand up. "Backtrack a bit. Grace?"

"From school. The shy one."

He vaguely remembered a Grace. She'd been quiet, smart, and had never spoken to him. "She's marrying a prince? A real prince?"

"As opposed to a fake one?" Paul said dryly.

Jeremy flipped him off playfully.

Chelsea barely noticed. She was too busy vibrating with excitement. "Yes, a *real* one. He's the Prince of *Talius*," she exclaimed, still glowing with excitement.

"I've never heard of it," Jeremy said skeptically.

Paul frowned. "Me either."

"I have. I read about them once in *Time*," she said, waving a hand dismissively. "It's somewhere near France. They won their independence after World War II, so they're fairly new to the world of diplomacy."

"If she's marrying a prince…what the hell is she doing *here*? I know she grew up here, but aren't there traditions and shit royal weddings have to follow?" he asked.

"That's what I said, but they want to keep it secret. His countrymen aren't happy he's marrying an American, so they want to do it here. We'll need security, and it's a rush wedding, so it'll be a little hectic, but we can totally do it. I mean, we planned our own wedding in two months, right? Why can't we do it again?"

Jeremy hesitated. "Right…"

Security. Princes. Would-be Princesses. Secrets.

This all translated to a hell of a lot of work.

And when you threw in the word "rushed," that made it even worse.

It was nice seeing Chelsea so excited, and he adored when she smiled like that, but realistically speaking, this sounded like an awful lot for them to handle so early in their game. They were just starting to make a name for themselves in the wedding industry. While this could be huge for them, if done correctly, it could also be catastrophic for them if they screwed it up.

Was that a risk they should take?

"Wait, was that Grace *Grigoris?*" Paul exclaimed, his eyes wide.

"Yes!" Chelsea beamed. "Crazy, huh?"

"Very. She barely even talked." Paul snorted. "How'd she snag a prince?"

Chelsea narrowed her eyes on him. "That's not fair. She's gorgeous—"

"How rushed are we talking here?" Jeremy interrupted before the two of them went off on one of their legendary O'Kane fights.

His wife stiffened, and slowly turned to him. "Well, it's imperative they do this quickly, because no one can find out, so you see, we have to really get on this right away, before the press—"

"Chels." He locked eyes with her, and she looked away. Shit, this was worse than he thought. She never looked away from him unless it was *bad*. "How rushed?"

"Two months." She bit her lip. "The wedding is penned in for July 30."

His blood rushed through his veins with a red hot fury, because if she was saying what he thought she was saying...

"Funny, because we aren't going to be here then. We'll be on our *own* honeymoon, which you promised me you would go on."

"Unless we aren't." She finally looked at him again. "Unless we push it back."

And that right there was why she wouldn't look at him earlier.

Son of a bitch.

ABOUT THE AUTHOR

JEN McLAUGHLIN is a *New York Times* and *USA Today* bestselling romance author. She was mentioned in *Forbes* alongside E. L. James as one of the breakout independent authors to dominate the bestseller lists. She is represented by Louise Fury at the Bent Agency. She loves hearing from her fans, and you can visit her on the web at JenMcLaughlin.com.

Looking to Fall in Love in Just One Night?
Introducing BookShots Flames:

**Original romances presented by James Patterson
that fit into your busy life.**

Featuring Love Stories by:

New York Times bestselling author Jen McLaughlin

New York Times bestselling author Samantha Towle

New York Times bestselling author Sabrina York

USA Today bestselling author Erin Knightley

Elizabeth Hayley

Jessica Linden

Codi Gary

Laurie Horowitz

…and many others!

Available only from

James Patterson's
BOOKSHOTS
Flames

"PLEASE DON'T LET ME FALL—AGAIN."

Since Siobhan Dempsey has made it as an artist, she's ready to
start a life in New York with the love of her life, billionaire
Derick Miller. But their relationship has been a roller-coaster ride
that has pushed Derick too far. Will Siobhan be able to win back
her soul mate?

Read the stunning ending to the Diamond trilogy, *Exquisite*,
available only from

ALSO AVAILABLE
DAZZLING: THE DIAMOND TRILOGY, BOOK I
RADIANT: THE DIAMOND TRILOGY, BOOK II

THE GOLDEN BOY OF FOOTBALL JUST WENT *BAD*.

Quarterback Grayson Knight has a squeaky-clean reputation—
except he's suddenly arrested for drug possession. Even though
she's on the opposing side of the courtroom, DA's assistant
Melissa St. James wants desperately to help him—and he
desperately wants her....

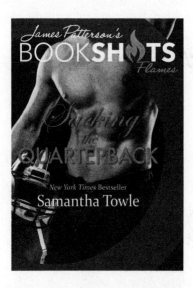

**Read about their thrilling affair in *Sacking the Quarterback*,
available now from**

SHE NEVER EXPECTED TO FALL IN LOVE WITH A COWBOY....

Rodeo king Tanner Callen isn't looking to be tied down anytime soon. When he sees Madeline Harper at a local honky-tonk—even though everything about her screams New York City—he brings out every trick in his playbook to take her home.

But soon he doesn't just want her for a night. He wants forever.

Read the playful romance,
Learning to Ride, **available now from**

"I'M NOT ON TRIAL. SAN FRANCISCO IS."

Drug cartel boss the Kingfisher has a reputation for being violent and merciless. And after he's finally caught, he's set to stand trial for his vicious crimes—until he begins unleashing chaos and terror upon the lawyers, jurors, and police associated with the case. The city is paralyzed, and Detective Lindsay Boxer is caught in the eye of the storm.

Will the Women's Murder Club make it out alive—or will a sudden courtroom snare ensure their last breaths?

Read the shocking new Women's Murder Club story,
The Trial, **available now only from**

BOOK**SHOTS**